'You can't be serious, Hugh.'

'Naturally I'm not propal marriage, or a p... union in name o... at a later date. B... you need to secu... what you want, is... value most in the world?'

'What do *you* get out of this extraordinary and rather sacrificial gesture?'

Hugh smiled. 'Come now, Kathryn, you of all people know I'm selfish to the core. I get you, of course…staying on as my personal assistant,' he added, taking rueful note of the moment of shock which had flashed through her eyes.

He'd been right. She wouldn't have let him blackmail her into his bed. This way was much better all round. She would still be in his debt. She might even begin to like him a little…

THREE RICH MEN

*When a wealthy man takes a wife,
it's not always for love…*

Meet Russell, Hugh and James,
three wealthy Sydney businessmen who've been
the best of friends for ages. They know each other
very well—including the reasons why none of them
believes in marrying for love.

While Russell and Hugh
have so far remained single, James is
about to embark on his second marriage.

But all this is about to change
when not just James but Russell and Hugh too are
driven to the altar. Have any of them changed
their minds about love—or are they ruthlessly
making marriages of convenience?

THE BILLIONAIRE'S BRIDE OF VENGEANCE:
Russell's story
THE BILLIONAIRE'S BRIDE OF CONVENIENCE:
Hugh's story

Coming in December:
THE BILLIONAIRE'S BRIDE OF INNOCENCE:
James's story

THE BILLIONAIRE'S BRIDE OF CONVENIENCE.

BY
MIRANDA LEE

MILLS & BOON®
Pure reading pleasure™

First published in Great Britain 2009
Harlequin Mills & Boon Limited,
Eton House, 18-24 Paradise Road, Richmond, Surrey TW9 1SR

© Miranda Lee 2009

ISBN: 978 0 263 87208 8

Set in Times Roman 10½ on 12¾ pt
01-0609-47059

Printed and bound in Spain
by Litografia Rosés, S.A., Barcelona

THE BILLIONAIRE'S BRIDE OF CONVENIENCE.

CHAPTER ONE

SEVERAL heads turned as the three men made their way into the main bar of the clubhouse. Other men as well as women glanced their way, their gazes carrying a mixture of envy and admiration.

It wasn't just because these three were rich. Most members of the Sydney Royal Golf Club were wealthy. The attention they instantly drew, especially from women, was more basic than that. Cavewomen had invariably been attracted to cavemen who could best protect and provide for them; physically blessed alpha males whose prepotent genes ensured strong offspring.

A modern woman might imagine she chose her mates differently; that she was attracted to other attributes such as kindness and a good sense of humour. Recent research, however, showed that was false thinking. Apparently, the most attractive quality a man could possess was tallness.

The male trio striding through the bar-room were all tall. If that wasn't enough to give them an advantage over most members of their sex, they were also handsome and dark-haired and, yes, very rich indeed.

The man who headed straight for the bar and who was obviously going to buy the first round of drinks was Hugh

Parkinson, only son and heir to the Parkinson Media fortune. Thirty-six years old, Hugh was Sydney's most eligible bachelor, a well-known man-about-town with a plethora of past girlfriends, none of whom—amazingly—had a bad word to say about him. A natural charmer, he devoted his life to the pursuit of pleasure, to remaining single and doing only as much work as strictly necessary.

His two golfing buddies were not cut from the same ilk. Both bordered on being workaholics, were married and had been moulded by past experiences into much tougher men.

Russell McClain owned McClain Real Estate, Sydney's most prestigious and successful property company.

James Logan owned Images, Sydney's most dynamic advertising and management agency.

The three men had been best friends since their school days. They knew each other very well, including their strengths and their weaknesses. Their affection for each other was genuine and unconditional.

Their Thursday-morning golf game, however, was a no-holds-barred affair. They always played for money, and they always played to win.

'What on earth's wrong with Hugh today?' James said as he and Russell settled at a table on the verandah overlooking the eighteenth green. 'Never seen him play such pathetic golf.'

'I have. When you were away, a few weeks ago, just before your wedding. I beat him hollow.'

'That's strange.'

'Thanks,' Russell said drily.

'You know what I mean. You're a pretty good golfer, but Hugh's better.'

'He should be. He practically lives on the golf course.'

'True.' James had used to play quite a bit himself, but not

so much since his marriage late last year. Or over the recent Christmas break, when his social calendar had been very full. 'Come to think of it, Hugh wasn't up to scratch last week, either. Only just managed to beat us. What do you think's responsible for his loss of form?'

'Not sure about lately,' Russell said. 'But back in November he was having some kind of woman trouble.'

James was truly taken aback. Hugh never had woman trouble. They threw themselves at his feet with regular monotony. He could have his pick.

'What kind of woman trouble?' James asked.

'I gather he fancied some piece who wouldn't come across.'

'Now, that'd be a first. Do you know who she was?'

'He didn't say. And I didn't ask.'

'Mmm.' James frowned as he watched Hugh weave his way towards the verandah with three beers cupped in his hands.

What could possibly be the reason for Hugh's uncharacteristic failure to bed a female of his choice? His womanising reputation, perhaps?

Nah. His being a bad boy with the opposite sex never seemed to put the girls off him. If anything, his being known as a rake only added to his appeal.

'On second thoughts, I've probably got it all wrong,' Russell said. 'He probably just had a late night last night, romancing his latest conquest. Maybe even the mystery girl herself. You and I both know that there isn't a girl alive who can resist those blue eyes once he turns on the charm. Except my Nicole and your Megan, of course.'

'Come now, he's not that irresistible.' But even as he said the words, James conceded that their friend was a veritable babe magnet.

'Hope you remembered to make mine a light,' Russell said

when Hugh placed the three glasses of beer on the table. 'I have to work this afternoon.'

'Me too,' James said.

Hugh pulled a face as he sat down. 'That makes three of us.'

'You're joking!' James exclaimed. 'You! Work? What's happened? Someone die?'

'Not quite. But close.' Hugh picked up his glass and downed a long, cool swallow of beer before continuing. 'Dad's off second-honeymooning with wife number five and I'm in charge of the ship.'

'Should we sell our shares in Parkinson Media?' James quipped.

Hugh shrugged. 'I shouldn't think so. No one could make worse business decisions than dear old Dad when he's consumed by unbridled lust. Who knows? By the time he comes back down to earth and wants to take the helm again, I might have recouped a few of the billions he's frittered away in the name of love. You might have forgotten, Jimmy boy, but I was dux of our school. I also graduated from uni with honours degrees in economics and corporate law. I'm not just a pretty face, you know.'

'Now we know why your mind wasn't on your golf today,' said an enlightened Russell. 'So when did all this happen?'

'Last weekend.'

'No wonder you're looking a bit frazzled. I'll bet it's a long time since you've done a full day's work.'

'It's been a while,' Hugh admitted, not willing to confess that there'd been a few weeks leading up to Christmas last year when he'd gone into the office almost every day and worked his silver tail off.

The reason for this episode of uncharacteristic diligence had been extremely perverse: his PA.

Hugh hadn't realised when he'd hired Kathryn Hart several months earlier that he might one day find her so damned sexy.

She wasn't conventionally beautiful, certainly not pretty. Her facial features were too large, her cheekbones too high and her mouth too wide. He also hadn't noticed her voluptuous figure at the time of her one and only interview. He'd been concentrating solely on what was contained in her excellent résumé.

Of course, he'd been in a bit of a rush at the time, his father's decision to place him in charge of the publishing arm of Parkinson's having come right out of the blue. Hugh hadn't anticipated taking over anything till his father expired. Whilst Richard—Dickie—Parkinson had made sure over the years that his son and heir had had a sprinkling of experience in every facet of his very diverse company, he was not the kind of man to give over power easily.

Surprisingly, Hugh had not been pleased at this unexpected responsibility.

Not willing to totally give up the easy-going lifestyle he'd become accustomed to, Hugh had immediately sought an assistant with superb skills in the publishing field, someone competent and decisive who could cover for him when he wasn't in the office. Kathryn Hart had seemed perfect, a cool customer who wasn't in any way flirtatious with him, as some of the other candidates had been.

He hadn't anticipated that Miss Capability would practically bully him into doing the job entrusted to him, or that he would become increasingly consumed with unwanted desire for her.

That was the perverse part. Because there wasn't anything he could do about his feelings for her.

Why? Because by the time he realised he fancied her, she was engaged. Shortly to be married, in fact.

Although Hugh was considered a conscienceless rake by all and sundry, the truth was he was quite sensitive to other people's feelings and would never pursue another man's woman. Sex, for him, was high on his list of life's little necessities. But only when it came *without* complications or consequences.

If Kathryn had been free, Hugh would simply have seduced her, making his daily trips to the office events to be anticipated with pleasure, not dread. As it was, he was forced to endure his growing desire for his PA with a level of physical frustration previously unknown to him. He'd even lost interest in other females, suddenly finding them boring in the extreme. There was only one woman he wanted right now.

And for the first time in his life, he couldn't have her.

'Have you moved into your dad's penthouse as well?' James asked.

Hugh shook his head. 'He offered. But I declined. I prefer my own place at Bondi.'

Which he'd bought several years earlier with money he'd accumulated on the stock market, with no help from his father, financial or otherwise. He'd used the cash he'd earned fruit-picking during several summers in his university years when his friends had thought he was overseas, skiing in Europe. Instead, he'd been working his way around Australia, proving to himself that he didn't need his father's money to survive and that he was capable of working just as hard as anyone else.

It had been a male-pride thing.

His recently refurbished and now extremely valuable apartment overlooked Bondi Beach, and was within a hundred metres of the rock pool in which he swam most mornings, come rain, hail or shine. It was the perfect bachelor pad, not too large, but with everything a single man could desire.

The thought of living in his father's oversized, over-luxurious and rather soulless penthouse held no appeal whatsoever, despite it being in the same city skyscraper as the offices of Parkinson Media.

'But it'd save you a drive into the CBD every day,' James said. 'You'd never be late. That should please that slave-driver of a PA of yours. The one who's always calling you. What's her name, now?'

'Kathryn,' Hugh said, suppressing a shudder at the thought of never being late. Being late was the only power he had over that witch.

Punctuality was a real issue with Kathryn. He knew it got under her skin whenever he was late.

Which reminded him...

Hugh glanced at his watch. It was almost noon. There was a meeting of the board this afternoon. He really couldn't be late for that. The other directors would think him not only rude but also not fit to be CEO, even temporarily. It would be foolish of him not to try to make a good impression.

Thankfully, he'd had the forethought to move some clothes into his father's penthouse, so that he could shower and change there when necessary. He wouldn't make a good impression wearing casual trousers and a short-sleeved golf shirt.

'Sorry, chaps,' he said, downing the rest of his beer in one swallow. 'Can't stay. Important meeting this afternoon.'

Hugh had to smile at the expressions on his friends' faces. But his smile faded once he reached his car, his mouth twisting into a grimace as he climbed in behind the wheel and started the powerful engine.

In fifteen minutes he would be in Sydney's CBD—the central business district. In less than twenty, he would be back in the lion's den.

Hugh slammed the Ferrari into gear and accelerated away, torn by the feelings which swamped him. One part of him—his masochistic side, obviously—wanted to be with Kathryn. His more sensible side knew he could not go on like this. One day, something was going to give and he would make a big fool of himself. And possibly find himself on the end of a sexual harassment charge.

The only logical solution was to get rid of the woman.

But how?

Hugh had racked his brain to find an excuse to get Kathryn out of his life—and out of his sight—once and for all. But she was capable and conscientious and didn't make mistakes, never arriving late or leaving early. She was the epitome of PA perfection.

His being elevated to temporary CEO of Parkinson Media had not fazed her. Kathryn had slid into the role of top secretary in the company without turning a hair, his father's hard-working PA having been given much deserved leave whilst her boss was off, gallivanting around the world.

One of Hugh's remaining hopes was Kathryn's marriage in five weeks' time.

Not that she was having a long honeymoon. She was not going to be that kind to him. Miss Must-Not-Waste-Money Hart was tying the knot on a Friday evening in a small, celebrant-officiated ceremony, then spending a whole two days honeymooning in a hotel in downtown Sydney before returning to work first thing on the Monday morning!

Hugh's other hope rested on Kathryn's becoming a mother. He knew she was turning thirty next birthday, that age when a woman became very aware of her biological clock. No doubt she would start trying for a baby straight away. She'd expressed the wish over coffee not long back that she wanted two children, a boy first, then a girl.

Lord knew how she was going to manage that! But if anyone could, it would be Kathryn. Her whole life seemed to be planned out with set time schedules and goals. Hugh was already praying for the day when she'd come into the office and announce that she was pregnant.

Though a pregnancy would not be the immediate end of his problems, of that he was sure. He had no doubt that Kathryn would work right up to the baby's birth. She was that kind of girl.

The kind of girl, too, who would look even sexier pregnant. Her already impressive bosom would become even more lush, her wide, child-bearing hips accommodating a baby easily with only the most minimal bump.

He could see her now, positively glowing with health and hormones. And he could see himself wanting her all the more.

The prospect horrified him.

Hugh's teeth clenched hard in his jaw. Could he endure at least another year of this?

He would have to, he supposed. What else could he do?

There was one thing he *could* do. Eventually. Offer her a very generous maternity leave. Six months with full pay. Twelve months, if necessary.

No, that would be extremely difficult to explain. Six months was all he could get away with. Hopefully, by then, she would be so enamoured by her son—it would be a boy, of course—that she wouldn't want to return to work.

Oh joy, oh joy!

Meanwhile, he had to find other ways to handle the situation, and minimise the effect Kathryn had on him.

The most obvious solution was to get himself a new girlfriend, some hot little number. There was no shortage of candidates. Maybe, if he chose a busty brunette, he could pretend she was Kathryn and cure some of his frustration that way.

Sydney's CBD came into view and Hugh's stomach automatically tightened. He hoped she wasn't wearing that infernal black suit today, the one with the jacket which nipped in at her tiny waist and the skirt which hugged her curvaceous rear just a little too tightly; the one he'd been wanting to rip off her from the first day when she'd walked into the office wearing the wretched thing!

No such luck, he realised within seconds of striding into the suite of rooms which he'd nicknamed the lion's den many years earlier. At the time he'd been referring to his father as the lion, always roaring at everyone. Now the lion was a different sex.

Kathryn didn't roar, but she could be just as intimidating.

Hugh tried not to bristle when she glared pointedly at her watch, then at his clothes.

'Surely you're not going to the board meeting this afternoon dressed like that,' she said coolly.

Hugh covered his annoyance by shooting her what he hoped passed for a drily amused smile. 'Kathryn, even I wouldn't have the gall to do that. I'm just going to pop up to Dad's penthouse where I intend to change. I brought some clothes over last Sunday with this kind of thing in mind,' he added before she asked him what into.

'Up there for thinking,' he said, tapping his temple and thoroughly enjoying the flash of surprise which had zoomed into her normally unflappable grey eyes. 'Meanwhile, order me a club sandwich, would you? You know what I like. And some coffee. Ask them to deliver it in…' he glanced at his Rolex '…twenty minutes,' he finished brusquely before striding into the inner sanctum, grateful for the private lift which would enable him to go up to his father's penthouse without having to walk past his PA one more time.

CHAPTER TWO

KATHRYN counted to ten under her breath before phoning through the lunch order, all the while endeavouring to calm her rapid pulse-rate and bring her inner self into line with her more composed outer façade.

But honestly, if ever there was a man designed to irritate her to death it was Hugh Parkinson!

She'd initially been reluctant to apply for the job as his PA. She didn't think much of men born with silver spoons in their mouths. Didn't think much of working for them, either. One of her earlier bosses had been born rich and had been presented with running one of his doting grandfather's newspapers when he'd been all of twenty-four. Talk about bone idle!

Still, she'd learned a lot from having to practically do his job for him. Learned, too, that rich young men often had wandering hands. After leaving that job, she'd chosen her employers more carefully, steering well clear of smarmy but usually good-looking creeps with more money than morals. It was only natural, then, that she'd be wary of working for the richest, possibly best-looking creep in all of Sydney!

The thought of that wonderful salary he'd been offering, however, had seduced her into putting in an application.

To give Hugh Parkinson some credit, he'd conducted her

interview in a very businesslike manner. She'd been quietly impressed, to be honest. And very flattered when, after a most intense twenty minutes of questioning, he'd told her that she was just what he was looking for and hired her on the spot. She'd congratulated herself at the time on reading the situation well and dressing down a little for the interview. Not too much make-up, hair pulled back into a French roll, jewellery very basic. And a navy pinstriped trouser suit which had become a little looser since she'd started going to the gym.

She'd imagined—probably rightly so—that a lot of girls might have presented themselves more glamorously, hoping to use sex appeal to get the job. Hugh Parkinson did, after all, have a reputation as a ladies' man.

There'd been not a hint of flirtation in his manner, however, and she'd been prepared to concede that perhaps the tabloid Press had it all wrong. He wasn't a playboy, she'd decided that day. He was a serious businessman whose bachelor status and movie-star good looks made him an easy target for salacious stories about his love life.

It wasn't till afterwards—about a month into the job actually—that she discovered how wrong she'd been. Hugh was just what he'd been depicted as: just like that other boss of hers, he hadn't wanted an assistant. He'd wanted her to do his damned job for him whilst he was off having five-hour lunches and playing golf and who knew what else with the never-ending number of women who bombarded the office with calls running after him!

Well, she hadn't been having any of that. Not a second time. So she'd informed him, as tactfully as her indignant fury would allow, that the editors of Parkinson's many magazines—the ones he was supposedly in charge of—didn't want to deal with his secretary. They wanted him—their boss—to be there to talk to, and run ideas by, and to make the many decisions which had to be made on a daily basis.

When he still hadn't shown up at work on a regular basis she'd rung him continually, badgering him over the phone till it had probably been easier for him to spend at least a few hours in the office every day.

Which should have made her happy.

But oddly, it hadn't.

His increased presence gradually began to grate on her nerves, she wasn't sure why.

So had Daryl's never-ending jealousy.

'No boyfriend wants his girlfriend working for a billionaire,' Daryl had complained soon after she'd started the job. 'Certainly not one with Hugh Parkinson's reputation. What if he makes a move towards you? What if he asks you to go away with him to a conference or something?'

She'd placated Daryl at the time, telling him that he was being silly, that she loved him and only him, and that she would never have her head turned by the likes of Hugh Parkinson.

Daryl had asked her to prove it by agreeing to marry him.

Kathryn had still been reluctant. Although she wanted marriage, underneath she was afraid of it. Afraid of trusting her life to any man. Over the years she'd had a history of falling for guys who'd proved to be less than perfect.

But then two things had happened to change her mind. Firstly, Val had finally succumbed to the cancer she'd been battling for several years. Not an unexpected event, but still very upsetting. Then Kathryn had received a letter from a solicitor shortly after Val's funeral, saying that Val had willed the beach house to her, provided she marry before she turned thirty. If she was still single on that date—which at that time had been a few months away—the house would be sold and the proceeds given to cancer research.

Kathryn had initially been shocked with her old friend for using emotional blackmail to push her into marriage. In the end, however, she'd been grateful to Val for forcing the issue and making her see common sense.

OK, so Daryl wasn't perfect. But then neither was she. If she kept waiting for Mr Perfect to come along, she would die a lonely old maid.

Initially, Daryl hadn't been too thrilled when she accepted his proposal. He'd accused her of not really loving him, of just using him to get her hands on a million-dollar property. Which was what the Pearl Beach weekender was currently worth. She'd soothed him by revealing that she had no intention of ever selling the house; that it was a place of great sentiment to her. He'd soothed her in return by taking her to bed and showing her why she'd fallen in love with him in the first place.

Once Kathryn had decided on marriage to Daryl, she'd embraced the idea one hundred and ten per cent, immediately making detailed plans for their future together. Naturally, she'd chosen the ring—Daryl might have picked something ridiculously expensive—*and* made all the arrangements, insisting that they have an inexpensive ceremony and reception—only ten guests—followed by an even more inexpensive honeymoon.

When Daryl complained about her miserliness, she'd explained that she wasn't going to waste any of her hard-earned savings on what was really just a party and an excuse for a holiday, both come and gone in a flash. She needed every cent for a decent deposit on a house here in Sydney.

Sydney was, after all, the most expensive city in Australia to live in. Houses came at a premium. So did interest rates.

She wasn't about to fall into the trap of having too large a mortgage which they wouldn't be able to pay back, once she left work to have a baby.

Neither she nor Daryl had well-off families to fall back on in times of financial difficulty. In fact, neither of them had *any* family to fall back on. Both of them had come from troubled, single-parent households. Each had seen what little close family they had finally being snuffed out through drink, drugs and disease.

But where Kathryn's background had formed her into a careful, highly organised, money-wise character, Daryl was more impulsive and not good with money at all. Still, he was very good at his job, being a top sales representative for a successful office-supplies company. His salary was excellent and he had a company car. Kathryn felt sure she could rein in his tendency to be extravagant, once they were married.

He was going to make a good husband and father. In time.

Right now, however, he was being a right pain in the neck, his jealousy not having been helped by her temporary promotion. Already he was complaining about the extra hours she was working. Last night, when she'd arrived home at seven-thirty—the preparations for today's board meeting had been endless—he'd demanded she hand in her notice.

'After we're married,' she'd hedged.

'You're just saying that,' he'd retorted. 'I know you. You like working for that rich bastard. You fancy him. I know you do.'

'Don't be ridiculous,' she'd snapped, tired of their endless arguments about her job and her boss.

'I'm not being ridiculous. I'm not blind, you know. He fancies you too. I saw the way he looked at you at the Christmas party.'

'Oh, for pity's sake!' she'd exclaimed with considerable

exasperation. 'Now you're being even more ridiculous! In all the months I've worked for Hugh Parkinson, not once has he ever done or said anything remotely out of line. He does not fancy me. Never has, never will.'

Which was probably what was adding to her irritation today, Kathryn accepted with a flash of feminine insight: Hugh's lack of male interest in her.

No girl liked to be looked straight through all the time the way Hugh did her, as if she was part of the wallpaper.

Not that any of the offices in Parkinson Media had wallpaper, especially this one. It was wall-to-wall wood panelling in here, totally different from the sleekly modern open-planned offices which filled the floors before. The big boss's suite of rooms was straight out of an élite English men's club, all the furniture antiques, the carpets richly patterned, heavy silk curtains framing the windows.

Kathryn's office-cum-reception area was ridiculously large, with a plush sitting space, along with its own powder room and cloakroom as well as a small kitchen where she could prepare coffee or tea. Her desk was a huge leather-topped slice of solid walnut with carved legs and more drawers than she could ever fill. The computer and printer occupied less than a quarter of the available work surface.

In truth, she preferred her other office and her other desk.

But she wasn't about to complain, not with the additional money she would earn over the next four weeks. She was already planning what she could buy with it: some extra-nice sheets, for starters, Egyptian cotton. She might be frugal by nature but she liked nice things. Quality things, that lasted.

Take her clothes, for instance. She didn't have a huge wardrobe but she bought good clothes. Not top designer-wear, she couldn't afford that, but well-made suits and real silk shirts and camis in mix-and-match colours, along with genuine leather shoes and bags. None of that cheap vinyl stuff. Her jewellery was minimal but quality too, not too expensive since she preferred silver to gold.

She was admiring the delicately designed silver watch which she'd treated herself to at Christmas when the phone on her desk rang, the security man downstairs informing her that a delivery guy was on his way up with a food order.

'Not the same guy as yesterday,' he added. 'I had to give this chap instructions on how to get to your office.'

'Wow!' the spotty-faced youth exclaimed when he finally arrived. 'This is some place. The view must be fantastic!'

'Quite,' she said coolly. 'Thank you, Ken.'

'You know my name!'

She pointed to the name tag on his shirt pocket.

'Oh, yeah,' he said, flushing. 'I forgot. It's my first week. Not used to it.'

Mine too, she almost said to make him feel better. But didn't. She'd found it best, over the years, not to be too familiar with delivery guys. The older, better-looking ones didn't seem to need much encouragement.

After he left, Katherine carried the food into the kitchenette and arranged the oversized sandwich on a proper plate on a tray, whilst leaving the steaming coffee in its takeaway cup, Hugh liking his coffee very hot and very strong.

He rarely asked her to make him coffee, though she would have, quite happily. She wasn't one of those silly PAs who thought making coffee beneath her. She'd always understood that her job as a personal assistant was to assist her boss in any way she could. She didn't object to collecting his drycleaning, or buying presents for his mother. She didn't even mind covering for him, occasionally.

But only up to a point and only if he deserved it.

Hugh deserved no such consideration, she decided as she carried the tray into his father's super-huge office and placed it on the super-huge desk which sat in front of the super-huge window. The only son and heir to the Parkinson fortune was spoiled and lazy and never on time, she thought irritably as she glanced at her pretty watch and saw that twenty-five minutes had passed since she ordered his lunch.

So where was he?

She glared at the determinedly shut door on her far right, the one which looked like any of the wood-panelled doors which led into and out of the office. This one, however, concealed a secret alcove where there was a private lift to the penthouse above. You needed a special keycard to get into both, security a must for mega-rich men like Hugh and his father.

Kathryn almost gasped when that door was suddenly wrenched open and in strode her boss, looking breathtakingly handsome in a suit she'd never seen before, dark charcoal-grey in colour, with a single-breasted and superbly shaped jacket. The casually elegant style suited him. His dazzlingly white shirt highlighted his blue eyes, his olive skin and his dark brown hair, which looked extra-dark, since it was slightly damp.

And then there was his tie…

Hugh had a thing about bright ties. This one was scarlet and striped with silver…very eye-catching.

'So what do you think?' he shot at her as he walked behind the desk. 'Will I do?'

Kathryn kept her expression cool. If he expected her to rave about his appearance, then he had another think coming. Some kind of compliment, however, seemed reasonable.

'You look very…smart,' she said.

Hugh's eyebrows shot upwards. 'You mean, I have your seal of approval? For once,' he added with a wry laugh as he removed his jacket then draped it over the back of the large leather desk chair.

His partial undressing perturbed her for some reason. Silly, really. She'd seen him without a jacket often enough. She'd also witnessed him in casual clothes, even shorts on the day when he'd rushed into the office after spending the morning sailing on the harbour.

She already knew he had a great body, his tall, broad-shouldered frame not needing to be bolstered by excessive padding.

Perhaps it was the whiff of something spicy and exotic which the removal of his jacket had sent her way. She'd never smelled this particular cologne on him before and it was very…sexy.

'So is everything ready for this afternoon?' he asked her as he sat down, then swept one half of the club sandwich up to his mouth.

His eyes questioned her as he munched away with relish.

'I…I think so,' she said, annoyed with herself for sounding less than confident. But it was the first time she'd had to organise a board meeting, although Elaine had left her excellent instructions on her computer in a special file.

Everything Kathryn might need to know during the next month was on that computer. Elaine had also left behind her personal mobile number, in case she was in doubt about anything. Kathryn had given in and called her yesterday, just to check on a few things.

'Yes, everything's ready to go,' she reiterated more firmly. 'The boardroom's all set up for the meeting, with copies of all the monthly reports set out in front of each chair. Apparently, I don't have to take down any minutes—it's not a quarterly or annual general meeting. But Elaine suggested I still tape proceedings. She said I should also stay in the room in case any of the directors want anything, like coffee or tea. I will be putting jugs of iced water on the table shortly, along with the glasses. But Elaine said, if the meeting goes on too long, some of them will want something hot to drink. And possibly a biscuit or two. Of course, I won't be sitting at the table itself. I'll stay in the background.'

'Sounds like you have everything well in hand. As for the meeting going on too long, I'll do my best to make sure that won't happen. And afterwards?'

'I've arranged for finger food and drinks in the reception room next to the boardroom. I've hired the usual catering company. They'll arrive around four. You shouldn't be finished before that.'

He nodded. 'Excellent. What's your estimated time of departure for the directors?'

Kathryn shrugged. 'I'm not sure. I've never been to one of these before. You have, though, didn't you say?'

'Not for ages. From memory, it was the most ghastly bore.'

'I'm sure you'll handle it all extremely well,' she said. For all Hugh's faults and flaws he could schmooze anyone, if and when he chose to.

'A second compliment, Kathryn?' he said drily. 'Watch it or I'll think you're beginning to approve of me.'

As if, Kathryn thought tartly. 'It is not my job to approve or disapprove of you, Hugh,' she said coolly. 'As I have said before, my job is to help you do *your* job.'

'At which you are invaluable,' he said, picking up his coffee and watching her over the rim as he sipped.

His eyes—his very beautiful blue eyes—were not as carefree as usual. They bored into her, stripping her, not of her clothes but the self-contained façade which usually kept her safely immune to her boss's considerable charms.

Suddenly a fierce awareness of his sex appeal swamped Kathryn, making a mockery of the way she despised other women's often swooning reaction to him. She actually felt weak at the knees, a physical phenomenon which she'd never experienced before, and which brought a bitter taste of shame to her mouth. How could she possibly be attracted to him?

Her teeth clenched down hard in her jaw as she struggled to recover her usual calm. But the unwanted sexual responses which had just flooded her traitorous body had left her feeling flustered, and confused.

She did the only thing she could do, under the circumstances. Said she had something to do and left the room.

CHAPTER THREE

'THAT'S a great girl you've got over there.'

Hugh followed the direction of Max's eyes and his gaze landed back on Kathryn; something he'd been trying to avoid all afternoon. Not too difficult a task during the meeting itself when she'd chosen to sit in a chair in a corner behind Hugh's left shoulder.

At the moment, however, Kathryn was working the reception room, chatting away to a group of the more elderly directors, bringing a smile to even the stuffiest of the gentlemen.

'Yes,' he agreed. 'She is.'

'Better than Dickie's secretary. More intelligent. More stylish, too. I hope you're paying her well. You wouldn't want to lose her.'

'I'm afraid that might not be my call. Kathryn's engaged to be married.'

'So? Married women work all the time. She doesn't look the type to stay home and play happy families. She has too much chutzpah!'

Too much of everything, Hugh wanted to say as he stared at her once more.

'Really, Max?' he said instead, somewhat impatiently.

'How can you possibly glean the measure of a woman's chutzpah from across the room?'

'I was talking to her earlier and happened to make some critical remark about the recent rise in interest rates. She took me to task and told me in no uncertain terms that if I thought the reserve bank was wrong, I didn't understand the effects of inflation on the economy. She didn't pander to my position, my sex or my age. She said it as it is, without fear or favour.'

'Kathryn does have a tendency to speak her mind,' Hugh said drily.

Max chuckled in his beard. 'Sounds like just what the doctor ordered for you, young man.'

'Meaning?'

'Meaning I would imagine that the majority of the opposite sex panders to you something rotten.'

'That is a burden I have to bear,' Hugh remarked in droll tones. 'If you'll excuse me, Max, I really should mingle.'

It was a full hour later before Hugh accompanied the last of the directors to the lifts. When he returned to the reception room, the caterers had almost finished cleaning up and Kathryn was frowning down at the screen on her mobile phone.

'That's just so typical,' she muttered.

'Something wrong?' he asked.

Her head whipped up, her eyes showing a most uncharacteristic consternation at finding him there.

'No, not really. Daryl was going to take me out to dinner tonight. But…um…something has come up and he can't.'

Hugh couldn't imagine anything making him break a dinner date with Kathryn. Not if he was assured of having her for afters. Which her fiancé was. They did live together, after all.

'In that case, why don't I take you out to dinner?' he said, whilst thinking he was a masochistic fool.

Her eyes rounded as her finely arched brows lifted skywards.

Hugh could appreciate her surprise. He'd never offered to take her to dinner before. Or even lunch. The occasional coffee break in the café on the ground floor was the extent of their socialising outside the office. Other than last year's Christmas party, of course, which had been held in the ballroom of the Regency Hotel.

What a wretchedly frustrating night that had been. He could not stand seeing Kathryn with that good-looking smoothie she was engaged to. In the end, he'd zeroed in on the second sexiest girl in the room, the newest in the stable of attractive female lawyers his father invariably hired. He'd left the party earlier than he should have and taken Kandi— a name more suited to a hooker than a lawyer, in his opinion— to a room upstairs for the night.

And, whilst Kandi had proved to him that she would probably be a success in either profession, Hugh had not asked her out again.

That was the norm with him these days. One date per woman was all he could tolerate, his rampant desire for Kathryn having temporarily spoiled him for any other female.

'Don't tell me you're not hungry,' he jumped in before she could make some feeble excuse. 'You didn't eat a single bite of finger food that I could see.'

She shrugged. 'I'm not much into finger food.'

'I have to agree with you on that score. I prefer to eat sitting down. Come on. I'll take you to Neptune's.'

'Neptune's! But that's one of the most expensive restaurants in Sydney.'

His smile was wry. 'I think I can afford it, Kathryn.'

'But don't you have to book in advance? I've heard it's very difficult to get a table there.'

'Not so difficult on a Thursday night. And not if I ring now. It's only half-past six.' He didn't like to say that the *maître d'* at Neptune's would find him a table at any hour on any night, a perk of being a billionaire.

Which he was already, courtesy of his paternal grandmother, who, not impressed with her own son's string of wives, had willed her personal fortune in a trust for her grandson. By the time Hugh gained control of this trust at the age of thirty, his grandmother's superbly invested millions had more than quadrupled. Since then, under his own management, and despite some years of economic upheaval in the stock market, his personal fortune had increased, which gave him considerable satisfaction.

Hugh knew people thought him lazy. But he wasn't. He could work hard, when required. He worked very hard at doing things he enjoyed, like golf and sailing and, yes, sex.

Or he *had*, till recently.

It frustrated him to death that his extremely enjoyable lifestyle was being ruined by one very irritating female who couldn't even be persuaded to go to dinner with him!

Because she was going to say no. He could see it in her eyes.

'I'm sorry,' she said, confirming his guess. 'But I don't think that's a good idea.'

Damn it, but he really wanted her to say yes to him. Just this once! Even if it was only for a meal.

'It's not unusual for a grateful boss to take his PA to dinner, Kathryn,' he said in a brisk, businesslike fashion. 'I'm sure your fiancé wouldn't mind.'

Oh, yes, he would, Kathryn thought.

But she didn't like to say as much, didn't like to confess that Daryl had this jealous thing about her working for Hugh.

Kathryn was tempted to go, seriously tempted.

Neptune's! She'd never been there. She'd never dream of going to somewhere so expensive; eating in five-star restaurants had never fitted into her budget. Daryl knew better than to take her to a restaurant which wasn't bring-your-own, with reasonably priced meals. Tonight, they'd been planning to go to their local Chinese.

Kathryn suspected that Daryl's last-minute letting her down to go out drinking with his mates was a kind of punishment for her coming home late last night. He could be petty at times. And quite vindictive. It was a trait that worried her sometimes.

What would he do if she actually went to dinner with her boss, to a place like Neptune's? He probably wouldn't talk to her for a week. Or make love to her. He'd give her the cold-shoulder treatment, knowing full well how much that would hurt her.

She couldn't bear it when he shut her out.

Of course, if she didn't tell him where she'd gone, he would probably never know. His mates always drank at a hotel in Burwood, which was a fair way from the centre of the city. It was also highly unlikely that anyone in their small circle of friends would see her dining out with her boss in a place like Neptune's.

'I refuse to take no for an answer, Kathryn,' Hugh pronounced firmly.

'But I'm not dressed for going out to a fancy restaurant,' she protested. Though rather feebly.

'Rubbish. You look fine. Now, go get your handbag whilst I make the necessary call.'

A still hesitant Kathryn watched him fish out his latest, hi-tech mobile phone, the one which could do just about anything short of autopiloting a plane.

'Hugh, I don't think—'

'For pity's sake!' he interrupted with a flash of frustration in his eyes. 'I'm not asking you to go away with me for the weekend. It's just a simple bloody dinner.'

Kathryn felt somewhat chastened by her boss's outburst. He must think she was a fool, making such a big deal out of his really very nice offer.

'You're right. Sorry,' she said swiftly. 'Just give me five minutes to fix my face.'

Exactly five minutes later Kathryn was standing in the powder room, staring at her fixed face in the mirror and thinking she was, indeed, a fool.

She should have stood her ground. Should have said no thank you, I really need to be getting home. Instead, here she was, with her lips freshly glossed, her hair taken down, her jacket unbuttoned and her heart going like the clappers.

Never, till today, had Kathryn allowed herself to surrender even in the slightest to her boss's infamous charm. She'd kept herself immune by ignoring his good looks and focusing on the real man underneath.

He was a playboy: spoiled and superficial, without depth and possibly even without decency.

The passing parade of beautiful young women in Hugh's life so far indicated a lack of moral fibre which Kathryn found deplorable. She thought it even more deplorable that women continued to chase after him the way they did.

Sometimes she despaired of her own sex. Didn't they have any pride? Any common sense? Hadn't they worked out yet that bachelor playboys like Hugh Parkinson only used them as sex toys, disposing of them quite ruthlessly when they tired of their charms? There was no future with them. None at all!

It pained Kathryn that she could feel even the slightest excitement over going to dinner with such a man.

But she did, there was no denying it. Her cheeks were flushed and there was a definite glitter of excitement in her eyes. In the last few minutes she hadn't give Daryl a second thought. And now that she did, all she felt for her fiancé was a fierce resentment. He should not have put her in this awkward position. He should not have let her down. He should have taken her out to dinner, as they'd arranged.

'Shake a leg in there, Kathryn,' Hugh shouted through the powder-room door. 'The caterers have just left and I have a booking for seven. You wouldn't want us to be late, would you?'

Sarcastic devil, Kathryn thought, but with a smile pulling at her mouth.

It startled her, that smile. And worried her.

She could not go out there smiling at him. It just would not do! Neither would her hair being down. Too telling, that. And potentially humiliating. She could not bear the thought that Hugh might think she was attempting some kind of cheap flirtation.

'I'll just be another minute,' she called back. 'Having some trouble with my hair.'

Back up it went. Not in a French roll—that would take too long—but a knot, wound very tightly on at the back of her head, then anchored with pins. She buttoned her jacket up again, then grabbed a tissue and blotted her shiny scarlet lips into a more sedate red.

There wasn't much she could do about her racing heart. But then, he couldn't see that, could he?

CHAPTER FOUR

HUGH didn't know exactly what to expect once Kathryn finally came out of the powder room. But during the extra minute she took, he began picturing her performing one of those transformations when the office girl turns from virgin to vamp in the twinkle of an eye by shaking down her hair, popping on some screw-me shoes, then flooding herself with an exotic perfume.

No such luck, he realised when the door opened and out came the Kathryn he'd become very used to, the one who didn't actually need to do any of those things to turn him on.

What had taken her so long? he thought with a savage burst of irritation. Her hairstyle was slightly different, he supposed, though still scraped back severely from her face with not a single lock escaping its imposed prison. As he glared at her hair, he suddenly itched to run his fingers through it, to pull it down and spread it out over her shoulders. Her very naked shoulders, preferably.

Cool it, Hugh, came the sharp warning from that part of his brain which was not connected with his male hormones.

'The caterers gone?' she asked, glancing over his shoulder.

'Yep. No one left here but us. Come on, let's go.'

Hugh resisted the temptation to take her elbow on the way

to the lift. He could already feel himself hardening. This could get mighty uncomfortable. On top of that, Kathryn would not appreciate any physical familiarity. He knew enough about her to know that. Some women were touchers but she very definitely wasn't.

Again, perversely, he liked that about her. Liked the way she protected her personal space and her air of self-containment.

It was very sexy. *She* was very sexy. Hugh sometimes wondered if she was aware of her unusual brand of sex appeal, or if she'd ever exploited it.

Somehow he didn't think so, which made her even sexier to him.

Wrong train of thought, Hugh. Damn, damn and triple damn!

Kathryn shot him one of her cool little smiles as they stepped into the lift.

'The meeting went well, don't you think?' she said. 'Everyone I spoke to seemed very pleased, both by the company's progress…and with you,' she added.

Somewhat reluctantly, Hugh thought.

'You're very good with people, aren't you?'

How she managed to make even a compliment sound like a criticism, he had no idea.

'Must come from all the parties I've been to,' he said off-handedly as he pressed the car-park button. 'By the way, Max was extremely impressed with *you*. He thoroughly enjoyed your lecture on inflation.'

Her head whipped his way, her eyes showing concern.

'I'm not teasing you,' he said. 'I'm being serious. He liked you. Said I was to do everything in my power to keep you. Which leads me to my next question,' he added just as the lift doors opened at the basement level.

'Oh? What's that?'

'Do you intend to stay on working for me after you're married?'

She didn't have to say a single word, he saw the truth in her eyes.

'I see,' he said, astounded at his reaction to this news. Where was the relief? All he felt was dismay. Yet that was ridiculous! If he couldn't have her, then it was far better that she go. Out of sight would be out of mind. He'd be able to get back to normal. And next time, he'd be very careful over the kind of female he hired as his assistant. Maybe someone like his father's PA. Elaine was in her early fifties, a career spinster who'd been with Parkinson Media for yonks.

Clearly, his father was no fool. Or perhaps it was a case of once bitten, twice shy? His father's first wife, Hugh's mother, had once been his personal secretary. Of course, she'd been very pretty.

Hugh stared at Kathryn, who could hardly be described as very pretty. Yet she had a face which he was finding increasingly attractive, with its fine eyes and wide, sensual mouth. And then there was her figure, that tantalising, hourglass figure which was his constant torment.

'And when were you going to tell me?' he ground out, as—against all common sense—he cupped her elbow and steered her forcibly from the lift.

Kathryn was taken aback by his obvious anger. It wasn't like Hugh to be angry, about anything! As a boss went, he was extremely easy-going, *too* easy-going. Life was meant to be enjoyed, he'd once told her when she'd chided him over spending so much time out of the office.

His anger upset her. As did the way he was pushing her along. Heavens, but his grip was strong. It had to be down to all that golf!

'I didn't say I was definitely leaving,' she said with a degree of indignation. 'I haven't made up my mind yet.'

'That's not like you. I got the impression you had your life all planned out down to the last minute.'

How boring he made her sound. Boring and predictable.

'There's nothing wrong with having plans and goals,' she countered defensively. 'Not everyone can afford to just swan along without thinking about tomorrow.'

'*Touché*,' he said with the kind of light-hearted laugh she was used to hearing from him. It relaxed the tension which had been gathering in her stomach. So did his finally dropping her elbow. She hadn't liked him touching her like that, hadn't liked the funny little thrill it gave her.

It wasn't till Hugh bent to open a car door that she noticed they'd come to a halt next to a bright red sports car.

Like lots of women, cars held little attraction for Kathryn. All she required of a vehicle was that it be kept spotlessly clean and got her safely from point A to point B.

Hugh's car *was* spotlessly clean. Its metallic paintwork fairly shone. But it didn't shout safety at her, it shouted danger, excitement and, yes, sex.

In a jolt of sudden insight, Kathryn understood why rich playboys drove cars like this, and why other men coveted them. They were, quite simply, seduction on wheels. Even the act of lowering herself into the passenger seat felt flirtatious, with her skirt riding halfway up her legs. When Hugh didn't close the passenger door straight away, she glanced up to find him staring down at her provocatively exposed thighs.

It seemed an eternity before his gaze lifted from her legs to her face; an electrifying and exquisitely exciting eternity.

His eyes, when they met hers, betrayed no such excitement. A hint of irritation perhaps. Nothing more.

'Watch your elbow,' he advised brusquely before slamming the door shut.

'Foolish girl,' Kathryn muttered under her breath, gripping her handbag tightly in her lap whilst her billionaire boss strode round the front of the car.

But it was difficult to relax after being rattled so soundly by such a small thing as Hugh looking at her legs. Difficult to ignore her still thudding heartbeat. Difficult to pretend that she hadn't wanted him to go on looking at her legs.

He wrenched open his door and slid in behind the wheel.

'You haven't been in my car before, have you?' he threw at her as he leant forward and inserted his car key.

'No,' came her taut reply. There'd been no reason for him to drive her anywhere.

'Seat belts would be good,' he said with a sideward glace.

Kathryn cursed herself when she fumbled with hers and it snapped back over her left shoulder.

'Here. Let me,' he said, and leant over to do it for her.

She knew his arm brushing against her breasts was accidental but it didn't stop her nipples from tightening inside her bra—or the sharp intake of breath which accompanied this not-to-be-ignored evidence of sexual arousal.

'Sorry,' he muttered, no doubt thinking her gasp was a form of protest. 'There's not a lot of room.'

Once her seat belt was fastened, Hugh turned his attention to slipping his own belt on then starting the car, giving Kathryn the opportunity to gather her senses.

Any relief was short-lived, however, when the car's powerful engine throbbed into life, its vibration entering her body through her feet and shooting upwards, bringing a tingling to her whole body. When Hugh reversed out and accelerated away, taking the car-park corners faster than she ever would, Kathryn experienced a most uncharacteristic surge of exhilaration.

Normally, she despised speeding. But nothing was normal right now.

In no time they were out in George Street, where the steady lines of city traffic brought a swift halt to any speeding.

'So what do you think of my car?' he asked when they stopped at a set of lights.

What did she think? She thought it was so sexy it was sinful. But not as sexy as its owner.

'Very nice,' she said, and he laughed.

'Only you would call a Ferrari nice.' The lights changed and he was off again, this time a little more quickly, as the traffic ahead was thinning. He zapped left at the next corner, then right, after which she lost total track till he zoomed into a small car park down near the quay and braked to a halt.

'Have you been to Neptune's before?' he asked as he retrieved his car key then unsnapped his seat belt.

'No.'

'You'll like it.'

Kathryn was sure she would. How could you not like being taken to one of Sydney's most famous restaurants where the menu would be to die for and the wine like liquid gold?

Suddenly, Kathryn knew why all those women chased after Hugh.

Not necessarily to marry him—although most would, if they could. But because billionaires could show a girl a very good time. It was a case of *la dolce vita* to the max: the best cars, the best restaurants, the best holidays.

Men like Hugh could give a woman everything she wanted.

Except commitment.

He'd be very good in bed, though, came the provocative thought.

Not that she'd ever find out. Hugh wasn't the slightest bit interested in her in that way. You didn't need to have a master's degree to work out what sort of women he took to bed, and she wasn't one of them.

The man himself wrenched open the passenger door at that precise moment and reached his hand down towards her. Kathryn really had no option but to take it.

This time, however, she was ready for her traitorous body's reaction to him. This time, there wouldn't be any silly gasping. She would keep her cool *and* her head…

When she put her hand in his, and his fingers closed around hers, Hugh had to use every ounce of his willpower not to show his feelings on his face. He'd been in an acute state of arousal from the moment he'd looked at her glorious thighs earlier on and envisaged how they'd feel wrapped around him. Then, when his arm had brushed against her breasts, he'd come within a hair's breadth of throwing caution to the winds and making a total fool of himself.

When she'd stiffened her back against the seat and made that strangled sound, he'd been saved from attempting what would have been no doubt a disastrous move. In the short drive since that decidedly dangerous moment, he'd managed to regain some common sense—and some control.

But his arousal remained, as did the perverse pleasure that just touching her again was giving him. Slowly he drew her up out of the car, revelling in the warmth of her hand, though not the flash of discomfort he glimpsed in her eyes.

Too bad, he thought, and held her hand even more tightly.

The sound of his cellphone ringing annoyed the hell out of him.

Not so his PA, who immediately withdrew her hand from his and turned to close the passenger door.

'Don't forget to lock your car,' she said coolly whilst he pulled his phone from his trouser pocket and flipped it open.

'Hugh Parkinson,' he said with a touch of weariness. But truthfully, what kind of masochistic maniac was he to invite Kathryn to dinner? Self-flagellation had never been his bag.

'Hugh, darling,' said a female voice. 'Have I caught you at a bad time?'

'Not at all, Mum. What's up?' he asked whilst pressing the car's automatic lock then slipping the key into his trouser pocket.

'I can't make lunch tomorrow. Sorry.'

'That's all right. We'll make it for the following Friday.' A while back, his mother had complained that they hardly ever saw each other these days, except at Christmas and his father's weddings, so they'd instituted a standard date to have lunch together every second Friday. Oddly enough, he'd got to know his mother better during those lunches than he could ever have imagined. They weren't just mother and son these days, they were good friends.

'I'll have to check my diary and get back to you on that,' she said. 'We might have to make it another day.'

'You shouldn't be such a gadabout.'

'You wouldn't want me to sit at home pining for your father, would you?'

'Did you ever do that?'

'Only for the first ten years. So where are you off to tonight, darling? No, don't tell me. Let me guess. You've found yourself a new girlfriend at last, and you're going to impress her with dinner at Neptune's.'

Hugh's eyebrows lifted. It seemed his mother knew him very well indeed.

'Not quite,' he replied. 'I'm taking Kathryn out to dinner as a reward for all her hard work today.'

'To Neptune's?' his mother persisted.

'Yes.'

'And she *agreed*?'

'Why not? It's all perfectly harmless.'

His mother laughed. 'You're anything but perfectly harmless, darling. Not when it comes to the women you fancy.'

Hugh was struck speechless.

'You thought I didn't know?'

Again, he remained silent.

'I never tell you what to do these days, darling. But I'm going to now. Men who sleep with their secretaries bring a lot of misery, mostly to the secretaries. Especially engaged ones. So take your mother's advice and keep it zipped up whilst you're around that lovely girl.'

'I'll do that,' he bit out.

'Good. I really like Kathryn. If you ever did anything to hurt her, I would be very cross.'

'Mum, I must go. We have an early booking.' So saying, he snapped his phone shut and looked at Kathryn.

'Mum can't make it to lunch tomorrow,' he said by way of explanation.

'What a shame. We always have a nice little chat when she comes to the office.'

'So I gathered. Look, why don't we both turn off our mobile phones for the next couple of hours? There's nothing worse than people ringing you during dinner.'

He watched her hesitate, but only for a moment, before she

opened her handbag and switched off her phone. Hugh smiled his satisfaction. Such a small victory, but it pleased him.

'Good,' he said and, masochistically taking her elbow once more, began shepherding her across the car park towards the restaurant.

CHAPTER FIVE

NEPTUNE'S was everything Kathryn had thought it would be: very classily decorated, with a magnificent view of Sydney Harbour and a mouth-watering menu that made her uncharacteristically indecisive.

But how did one choose between so many incredible dishes?

Incredibly expensive as well. She wondered what price the wine would be.

'Stop looking at the prices,' Hugh said after she'd been staring at the menu for a full five minutes. 'I don't give a damn what you order. Just hurry up. I'm starving.'

Still, she dilly-dallied.

'Why don't you let me order for you?' he said somewhat impatiently.

'Perhaps that would be best,' she agreed when a waiter materialised at the side of their table.

Hugh told him they were skipping the entrée and going straight to the main course, selecting baby Barramundi, accompanied by an exotic concoction of pasta and vegetables, which she didn't dare ask the waiter to explain for fear she would sound ignorant. Hugh also ordered some herb bread—to be delivered quickly—and a bottle of red wine which she suspected cost a lot more than the fifteen-to-twenty-dollar specials she always bought from her local wine shop.

The waiter returned with the wine like a shot, Hugh taking his time over the taste-testing before giving his nod for the waiter to pour.

'I haven't tried this particular wine before,' he told her after the waiter departed. 'A friend recommended it to me. Tell me what you think.'

When Kathryn took her first sip, she literally sighed with appreciation. 'Oh, it's lovely.'

'I've had better,' Hugh said. 'But it's not bad. Aah, here comes our bread. And just in time. I'll need something to soak up the alcohol, if I'm going to drive you home afterwards.'

Kathryn almost spilled her wine. Which would have been a complete travesty. 'You don't have to do that,' she said hurriedly. 'I can easily take the train. I don't live all that far from the station.'

'You think I'd let you walk home after dark?'

'It doesn't get dark till after eight,' she replied, feeling grateful for daylight saving.

'Which it will be by the time we finish here. Don't make a fuss, Kathryn. And don't suggest a taxi. I'm driving you home and that's that. If you're worried I might be over the limit then don't be. I'll restrict my intake to two glasses and you can drink the rest.'

Kathryn found herself doing just that over the course of the next hour and a half, unable to resist either the wine or the wishes of the man sitting opposite her. Hugh in masterful mode was a force to be reckoned with. Her easy-going boss seemed to have changed today into someone she could no longer handle as easily, or ignore; someone she was suddenly finding devastatingly attractive.

Fortunately he didn't know that, and she aimed to keep it that way.

Nevertheless, Hugh's air of authority seemed to have robbed her of her willpower and turned her into the kind of woman who enjoyed deferring to her male companion. She'd even given in to his insistence that she have dessert, biting her tongue when he chose a calorie-laden piece of pecan and almond pie, complete with a diet-crushing dollop of whipped cream. Normally, she wouldn't have dreamt of eating such a thing. She had a tendency to put on weight very easily. Tonight, however, she'd savoured each delicious mouthful, washing it down with a lovely cup of Irish coffee, the bottle of wine having long been finished.

It wasn't till they were back in Hugh's Ferrari and hurtling along the western distributor, heading for home, that the first seeds of worry penetrated Kathryn's decidedly fuzzy head. What if Daryl had been trying to contact her tonight? What if, when he couldn't reach her on her mobile, he'd rung their flat and found no answer? What would he think?

Hopefully that she'd gone to the gym.

Kathryn comforted herself with the fact that Daryl didn't usually ring her when he went out with the boys. Still, it had been very silly of her to go to dinner with Hugh out of work hours. It broke one of her cardinal rules of never socialising with her boss, of never crossing that invisible line which marked them as employer and employee.

Not that she was ever in any danger of Hugh making a pass over dinner, or afterwards. Kathryn was well aware he wasn't attracted to her in that way. It was her own silly self which worried her.

In hindsight, she had to admit that all day she'd been very aware of him as a man, not her boss—for instance, when he'd come back down to the office dressed in that gorgeous suit. Then during the meeting, where he'd been extremely impressive. But, mostly, when he'd swept her out of the office and into his car in that wonderfully masterful fashion.

After tonight, she'd have difficulty looking at him and not remembering the way she'd felt when he'd leant across her body in the car. Her head might still see him as a lightweight womaniser with more money than morals, but her body was suddenly on a different wavelength, one which was secretly wishing for more. More rides in his car, more bottles of French wine, more of the envious glances the other women in that restaurant had bestowed upon her when they left together.

It was all insane and not conducive to a happy working life.

Kathryn decided then and there to start looking for a new job tomorrow. Now, *that* should please Daryl!

'You'd better give me directions,' Hugh said. 'I know you live in Ashfield but I don't get out this way very often.'

'I don't imagine that you do,' Kathryn remarked more acidly than was polite. But she refused to feel guilty. She had to work for this man for a few weeks still. The sooner she got their relationship back to the status quo, the better...

Hugh's mouth twisted into a wry grimace. Back to square one, he thought with a suppressed sigh. For a while there tonight, Kathryn had started acting like a normal woman. It must have been the wine which had temporarily softened her prickly attitude towards him back at Neptune's. That, or the good food. She'd certainly tucked in, visibly enjoying every mouthful. No wonder she had all those curves.

'Take the next exit,' she ordered brusquely. Which he did, following her crisply delivered directions for the next few minutes before turning down a wide street which was lined with Federation houses on the left and post-war-styled apartment blocks on the right.

'That's my place,' she said, pointing to a very plain, very square red-brick building on his right. 'Don't worry about turning round. Just drop me off at the next set of lights and I'll walk back.'

A natural born stubbornness—and a familiar burst of frustration—had him ignoring this last instruction and doing an abrupt U-turn and coming to a halt at the kerb right outside her building. It wasn't really a dangerous manoeuvre—the oncoming cars were some distance away—but he heard his passenger suck in her breath sharply…

Kathryn felt like hitting him.

'Sorry if I frightened you,' Hugh said with not a hint of apology in his voice.

She turned to glare at him. 'Road rules are there for a reason, you know.'

The eyes which met hers were unconcerned. 'There wasn't any danger. Besides,' he added, 'rules are meant to be broken.'

What an arrogant jerk you are, she thought.

'Please don't get out,' she said with icy politeness, and was out of the car in a flash. 'Thank you for dinner and for seeing me home. I'll see you in the morning. If you don't have another golf game, that is,' she added tartly just before slamming the car door.

Kathryn was still fuming when she let herself into her first-floor apartment. Resigning her job could not come quickly enough.

Throwing her handbag onto a chair, she glanced at the phone, glad to see that the red light on the answering machine wasn't blinking. No one had left a message, so Daryl hadn't rung here.

Undoing the buttons on her jacket, she walked into the bedroom. Only to stop in utter shock at the sight of Daryl, fully dressed and lying on top of the bed, his arms linked behind his head, his ankles crossed and his eyes wide open, fixed on her.

'Oh!' she exclaimed, her heart taking off at a gallop. 'What are you doing home so early?'

He didn't answer her. Instead, very slowly, he uncrossd his ankles and removed his arms from behind his head. Then he levered himself up off the bed, all the while watching her closely with cool eyes.

'I tried to ring you,' he said as he walked slowly towards her. 'But your mobile was turned off. Then I tried calling here. Still no answer. I was worried. So I came home.' He stopped in front of her. 'Where have you been?'

She almost told him the truth but something stopped her. Something in his eyes which frightened her into lying.

'I stopped in town after work for a bite to eat with one of the girls,' she said.

'Lying bitch,' he snarled, and slapped her hard across the face.

Kathryn cried out, both in pain and in shock.

'I *saw* you,' he snapped, 'getting out of his fancy car just now. You think I'm stupid. You think I didn't finally twig what's been going on?'

'N...nothing's been going on,' she stammered, her head spinning.

'You're a bloody liar! Men like Hugh Parkinson,' he spat, 'they always shag their secretaries. And let's face it, sweetheart, you like your sex. So is he good? Better than me?

Worth losing that precious weekender you so desperately want?'

Kathryn clasped her pounding head with her hands and just stared at the man she'd thought she loved and whom she'd thought loved her.

He laughed a cruel laugh. 'I see that it's finally sinking in what your little affair with your boss is going to cost you. Because no way am I going to marry you now.'

Kathryn's shock gradually gave way to outrage and anger.

'You think I'd want you to?' she threw back at him. 'I wouldn't marry you now if you were the last man on earth. You're lucky I don't ring the police and have you arrested for assault. But I will, if you hit me again. Trust me on that. Now I want you out of here. Tonight. Pack your things right now and go.'

'You can't make me do that!' he sneered.

'Yes, I can,' she countered furiously. '*I* signed the lease on this flat. *I* bought the furniture. Everything in this place is mine, except for your clothes. If you don't go willingly, I'll ring Hugh and have him send one of his bodyguards round to throw you out. He has several on his payroll.' This was a lie. Unlike his father, Hugh never used security. He said he'd rather risk being killed, or kidnapped, than live in fear.

'So you admit you're sleeping with that cocky bastard.'

'I'm admitting nothing.'

He glared at her, his eyes filled with hate and, yes, the threat of more violence.

'If you don't start packing,' she practically screamed at him, 'I'm calling the police.'

He scowled then spun away and stomped across the room to the wardrobe which held all his things.

Kathryn quickly moved round to the far side of the bed,

where she stood with her arms crossed, her face a stony mask. Inside she was trembling, shock once again rising to the fore. For all the problems that she'd had growing up, violence in her family had not been one of them. Daryl, though, had once confessed to her that his father had been physically abusive. Like father, like son. Kathryn was beginning to realise that she'd made a narrow escape tonight.

Not that the night was over yet. Hopefully, he wouldn't make any more trouble for her, or hit her again.

She watched in extremely tense silence whilst he stuffed his clothes into two bags, which she technically owned as well. But she didn't say anything. She didn't want to delay his departure.

Finally he'd emptied his wardrobe, glaring at her defiantly after he stalked into the living room and returned with several CDs.

'These are mine,' he growled as he shoved them into a side pocket of one of the bags. 'You gave them to me as presents. You can keep the engagement ring, of course. *You* bought it. No doubt you'll put it in a drawer till the next sucker comes along. Wouldn't want you to waste any of your precious money. God, I don't know what I ever saw in you! You're a cheapskate and a control freak. I guess your being a right little raver in bed blinded me to your true nature. But my eyes are well and truly open now.' With that, he swept up the two bags and headed for the door. 'I'll leave it up to you to cancel all the wedding arrangements, sweetheart,' he threw over his shoulder. 'Not that there's too many of them.'

Kathryn closed her eyes and remained where she was till she heard the front door slam. Then she ran to it, her hands trembling as she slid the internal security chain in place. That done, she hurried over to the coffee table, where she kept the telephone directory. Five minutes later she was talking to the receptionist of a twenty-four-hour locksmith company who promised to send someone round straight away.

By nine-thirty that evening, Kathryn was over two hundred dollars poorer, but at least Daryl would not be able to let himself in any time he wanted with the keys which she hadn't thought to demand from him. Aside from a very real fear that her now ex-fiancé might try to hurt her, she wouldn't put it past Daryl to return whilst she was at work tomorrow and clean the place out. The new deadlock would prevent that, along with the security bolts now fitted to all the windows.

It wasn't till Kathryn finished taking the necessary steps to make herself physically secure that her fragile emotional state finally caught up with her.

She didn't cry at first, but just sank down onto the floor where she happened to be standing, by the side of the bed. And there she sat for ages, her knees up, her arms wrapped tightly around her legs.

Alone again, came the blackly despairing thought. Alone in the world with no one to love her, no one to comfort her.

If this had happened a year ago, she would have left here and driven straight up to Val's place at Pearl Beach, to the one person who definitely had loved her, and the one place where she'd always found peace. And there, she would have healed. And found the courage to go on, as she had in times past.

But there was no Val to run to any more.

Any depression Kathryn had initially felt over the passing of her old friend last year had been partially lifted by the knowledge that, come her thirtieth birthday next month, she would take possession of Val's home. The thought that she could stay at this much-loved sanctuary whenever she wanted had soothed her worries over the future; had even given her the courage to accept Daryl's proposal and start making concrete plans to create a family of her own, something she'd always craved but which she'd feared as well. For what did she know of making a good marriage, or of being a good mother?

It seemed inevitable that any marriage she entered would eventually fail.

Kathryn did not like to fail at anything she did.

'Well, I've failed this time, haven't I?' she wailed aloud.

The thought of losing Daryl was not why her chin began to wobble. She'd already come to the conclusion he wasn't worth tears. It was losing Val's place which devastated Kathryn.

Never again would she walk up onto that sweet little verandah, or sit there watching the waves ripple gently onto the golden sand. Never again would she make tea in Val's large, comfy kitchen, or enjoy the wonderfully dreamless sleeps she had when staying there.

'Never again,' she choked out, the irrevocable words reinforcing the enormity of her loss.

It was then that she started to weep, huge, noisy sobs which racked her body and shattered her mind. Eventually, when she could weep no more, she clawed her way up onto the bed and collapsed on the quilt. Sleep came through sheer exhaustion, Kathryn not waking till the dawn light crept through her bedroom window.

CHAPTER SIX

HUGH stared at Kathryn.

He'd spotted the nasty bruise on her cheek the moment he'd strode into the office—half an hour late. He'd listened to her struggle to explain how she'd acquired her injury, and he'd watched, shocked, when she'd finally burst into tears.

'Oh, just go away,' she sobbed as she snatched a handful of tissues from the box she kept on her desk.

Hugh wasn't going anywhere. He would have liked to take her into his arms, but he knew that would be a fatal move. Instead, he stood patiently in front her desk and waited till her sobs subsided.

'You can't possibly marry that man now, Kathryn,' he said at last.

'I've got no intention of marrying him,' she snapped with some of her usual spirit. 'I threw him out.'

'And he just went?' It seemed unlikely to Hugh that a physically abusive fiancé would go meekly into the night.

'He wasn't going to. But I threatened him with the police. Then with one of your bodyguards.'

'But I don't have any bodyguards!'

'He didn't know that.'

'Mmm. He might come back, you know.'

'I did think of that, so I had the lock changed, straight away.'

'Very sensible,' Hugh said. 'But I think it would be wise if you stayed somewhere else for a few nights.'

Meanwhile, he aimed to find that bastard and give him a taste of his own medicine. Hugh had taken martial arts lessons when he'd been growing up, one of the many athletic skills he'd acquired during school holidays when his father had been too busy to spend time with him, and his mother hadn't known how else to cope with his endless energy.

'I don't think that's necessary,' Kathryn said.

'Well, I do. What good will you be to me if you come in here every morning, exhausted from not sleeping? I'll tell you what—you can stay in Dad's penthouse till he gets back. He won't mind.'

'I can't do that!'

'Why not?'

'Because…because…I just can't!'

'Rubbish. You'd be a lot tidier than me, and he said I could stay there. We'll go get some of your clothes right now. Then you won't have to go home tonight.'

Kathryn jumped to her feet, her face pained. 'You're doing it again.'

'Doing what?'

'Riding roughshod over me, like you did last night. I…I didn't want to go to dinner with you. Not really. You just wouldn't take no for an answer. Then I didn't want you to drive me home. But you insisted. If you hadn't, Daryl wouldn't have gone off his brain with jealousy, I'd still be getting married and I wouldn't have lost the thing I most value in the world!'

Hugh gaped at her. 'I can't believe you just said that,

Kathryn. You value a man who hit you more than anything in the world? I would have thought a woman of your character and common sense would despise such a coward.'

'I'm not talking about Daryl. I do despise him.'

'Then what? I'm totally confused.'

Kathryn's sigh sounded weary. 'It's a long story,' she said, and sank back down into her chair.

'We have all day.'

'We're supposed to be working.'

Hugh shrugged. 'I'm the big boss now, remember? I can do what I like. What say you put on the answering machine and we'll go have coffee somewhere?'

'No,' she said firmly. 'I don't want to do that. I…I don't feel like going anywhere in public. Not looking the way I do today. It was bad enough on the train this morning with everyone staring at me.'

'Yes, of course,' he said swiftly. 'I didn't think. At the risk of your accusing me of riding roughshod over you again, we could go up to Dad's penthouse and enjoy a cup of his truly excellent coffee out on the terrace. He has this great coffee machine up there which practically makes it for you.'

At any other time on any other day, Kathryn would have said no to that as well. But today she wasn't her usual strong-minded self. She felt fragile, and weak and, yes, needy.

'All right,' she said, her chin beginning to wobble once more.

His glance carried alarm. 'You're not going to cry again, are you?'

She almost laughed at the look on his face. 'No, Hugh. I'm not going to cry again.'

'Thank God,' he muttered. 'Come on. Let's go.'

Dickie Parkinson's penthouse was a showpiece, not a

home, with huge, open-plan living areas filled with the finest of Italian leather furniture, but no personal touches anywhere. The decorator had chosen black and white as the basic colour palate, giving the place a decidedly cold look. All the walls were white, so were the marble floors. The massive kitchen had shiny white cupboards with black granite bench tops and stainless steel appliances. The coffee machine Hugh had mentioned was black and stainless-steel combined. The mugs hanging on a steel rack next to it were black.

'Won't be long,' Hugh said as he switched on the machine and selected two of the mugs. 'Why don't you go out onto the terrace? Have a look around.'

She did as she was told, because it was better than staying with him in the kitchen and tolerating the same sexual awareness that she'd felt the previous day, and that had descended on her again during the ride up in the small lift. Thank goodness she had already decided to resign. This could get worse.

Maybe that would be a good idea anyway, common sense suggesting she move right away, to another state and another city. There was nothing to keep her in Sydney any more, certainly not this unexpected and highly unwanted attraction for a man whom she didn't despise as she now did Daryl, but whom she didn't respect.

It suddenly occurred to Kathryn as she stepped out into the sunshine that she had a habit of being attracted to handsome guys who had buckets of sex appeal, but who were, underneath, bad boys.

The terrace was much nicer than the penthouse. Firstly, the tiles underfoot were a warm cream colour, and the outdoor furniture made in a rich red wood. And then there was a roof garden, full of flowering bushes in all sorts of colours. Kathryn didn't know what the plants were called—gardening had never been part of her lifestyle—but that didn't stop her admiring them. The view was worth admiring as well, looking north across the city centre to the harbour bridge and beyond. The opera house was partially obscured by another building, but the quay was visible. The day promised to be warm, but at this hour the air was a pleasant twenty-three degrees, the sky a bright blue with just a smattering of cloud.

Kathryn sat down at a square table with four chairs, because that way Hugh couldn't sit down too close to her.

He was right. He didn't take long.

Kathryn tried not to stare as he carried two steaming black mugs towards her. But it was fascinating, in a way, how he was suddenly affecting her. All these months, she'd felt absolutely nothing in his presence. Well, nothing except irritation. Now there was a definite quickening of her pulse-rate as he drew closer.

Of course, he *was* drop-dead handsome. More so than Daryl, who'd been good-looking but not perfect, by any means. Bodywise there was simply no comparison. Hugh had it all. His face could not be faulted, either, his strongly masculine features softened by his sensual mouth and the way he wore his wavy, dark brown hair, flopping across his high forehead from a side parting. This style drew added attention to his eyes, which were a piercing blue, their impact heightened by darkly fringed lashes.

There'd been a time when Kathryn hadn't been in the least turned on by her handsome boss. But that time wasn't today.

'Hope I got it right,' he said as he placed the mugs on the table, then pulled out a chair. 'I know you drink it black but wasn't totally sure about the sugar content.'

'Two,' she told him.

'I got it right, then,' he said, smiling. 'So what do you think of Dad's pad?'

'I like the terrace, and the garden. But inside, it's a bit...um...'

'Soulless?'

Her eyebrows lifted. She hadn't been expecting him to say that.

'All Dad's houses are like that.'

'How many has he got?' she asked as she picked up her mug.

'Too many to count. The upkeep costs him an absolute fortune. But we haven't come up here to talk about dear old Dad. I want to hear that long story of yours. I'm intrigued.'

Intrigued was a good word, Hugh decided as he waited for her to stop sipping her coffee and start talking. Everything about Kathryn was beginning to intrigue him. He hadn't realised till today how little he actually knew about her. His knowledge of her life so far was limited to the facts on her résumé, plus what he'd garnered during their occasional coffee breaks together. He knew her father had died years before and her mother more recently. He knew she didn't have any brothers or sisters and something about her relationship with the horrid Daryl, of course. And about her marriage plans, which would not now, of course, be taking place.

Hugh tried to feel some guilt over his pleasure at Kathryn being suddenly single again, but failed. When he looked at her all he felt was a desire so intense that he sometimes wondered how she couldn't sense it.

'If I tell you,' she said at last, her tone taut and edgy, 'promise you won't judge me.'

Now he was even more intrigued.

'I can't imagine you doing anything seriously wrong, Kathryn.'

'Not wrong exactly...' She sighed. 'Look, to cut a long

story short, in July last year an old lady I knew died and left me her house in her will, provided I married by the time I was thirty. If that date passes and I'm still single, the house will eventually be sold off and the proceeds given to cancer research.'

Hugh was totally taken aback. 'Is that legal?'

'Apparently so. I did ask.'

'And?'

'It was around that time that I said yes to Daryl's proposal.'

Hugh frowned. 'Are you saying you never loved Daryl? That you were only marrying him to get your hands on this house?'

'See?' she snapped. 'I knew you'd think that.'

'What am I supposed to think?'

'I honestly thought I loved him,' she insisted fiercely.

'But you didn't.'

'I can see now that I probably didn't. I'm not heartbroken this morning. Not about him, anyway. Just about the…the…'

'The house,' he finished for her.

'Yes,' she said with a long, shuddering sigh.

'So where is this house?'

'Pearl Beach.'

Hugh's eyebrows arched. He'd heard of Pearl Beach. An artist friend of his had a holiday place up there. From what he gathered, it cost a lot to live there.

'I see,' he murmured.

'No, you don't,' Kathryn said irritably. 'You can't possibly. You don't know me. You have no idea why I would do such a thing. It has nothing to do with greed, or materialism. I would never sell the house. Never! Val knew that. It's…' She shrugged helplessly. 'Oh, what's the use? It's too late now.'

Maybe. Maybe not.

'Why do you think your friend made her will that way? Why didn't she just leave you the house and be done with it?'

Kathryn's face was pained. 'I think she was worried that I'd never get married. I've always planned to, but I always found it hard to take that final step, to commit myself for life to one person. I guess, deep down, I wasn't confident that I could make a marriage work.'

'I know how you feel,' Hugh said drily.

Her glance was sharp. 'Yes, I can imagine. Anyway, I took Daryl up to meet Val the Christmas before last and she liked him. Believe it or not, he can be very sweet and charming when he wants to be. She said that it was obvious we were right for each other and I was a fool if I didn't marry him. I said that I would, eventually, but maybe she didn't believe me. That's the only reason I can come up with.'

'Sounds logical. So why *does* this house mean so much to you?'

She shook her head from side to side. 'You'd never understand.'

'Why not?'

Her smile was wry. 'You just wouldn't.'

'Try me.'

'Let's just say that this house is to me what Tara was to Scarlet O'Hara.'

Hugh wasn't quite sure what that meant. He'd never read *Gone with the Wind* or seen the film. But he would, as soon as he could get a copy of the DVD.

'I first went there when I was nine,' she went on, her eyes clouding over to a far-away expression. 'Val used to have children with special needs for holidays. She was...very good to me. After I grew up, I used to go there whenever I needed emotional comfort and peace. It was my sanctuary. I'm not sure how I'm going to be able to cope in the future without it. But I guess I'll just have to. Life does go on.'

She picked up her coffee and took a couple of swallows before putting it down again, her eyes clear and cool once more. 'Hugh, I'm sorry, but I'm going to have to resign.'

'Resign!' Hugh wasn't one to panic easily but he was close to it at that moment. 'Why in hell would you have to do that?' he argued. 'You're not getting married now. There's no reason for you to resign.'

Her face betrayed definite agitation. 'There's nothing here in Sydney for me any more, only bad memories and…and…well…look, I just need to get away. You won't have any trouble filling my shoes.'

'Oh, yes, I will,' he said with dark irony.

'No, you won't,' she insisted. 'I'll work out my notice, give you plenty of time to find another PA.'

'I don't want you to leave,' he said, fixing his eyes firmly on hers.

She flushed. 'I'm sorry, but I have to.'

'You don't have to. You're choosing to.'

'All right,' she said with the defiant tilting of her chin. 'I'm choosing to.'

'The same way you chose to marry a man you didn't love.'

'That's not a very nice thing to say.'

'It's the truth.' She might not like admitting it, but it *was* the truth.

An almost ridiculous thought popped into Hugh's head, one which he immediately tried to banish. But it took hold, tantalising him, tempting him.

'If there was still a way by which you could acquire your friend's house,' he said slowly, 'would you do it?'

'What do you mean? What way?'

He could see the excited hope in her eyes, see that, yes, she might just go for his suggestion.

'You turn thirty...*when* exactly?'

She frowned at him. 'The twenty-third of February.'

'That gives us just over five weeks.'

'To do what?' she asked, and picked up her coffee once more.

'Get a marriage licence and get married.'

CHAPTER SEVEN

THE mug Kathryn had just picked up clattered back to the table, sending a great slosh of coffee over the rim.

'Oh!' she cried out, and hurriedly pushed back her chair as the staining liquid raced towards the edge of the table. Luckily, it missed her skirt and dripped down onto the cream tiles.

Her face, when she lifted it back to his, was flushed, her eyes quite angry. 'You shouldn't say crazy things like that!'

She was quite right, of course—it *was* crazy. But so was the driving sexual need which had been building in him these past few weeks. He had to have her. He *would* have her, through fair means or foul.

Still, Kathryn's reaction to his proposal suggested she was not about to say yes to his offer, a realisation which annoyed the hell out of him. All his life women had fallen into his lap. Why not this one?

He should have known she was not the sort of woman to allow herself to be blackmailed into bed. Still, that wasn't how he wanted her, was it? He wanted her warm and willing. Wanted her to look at him as he'd seen her look at that creep she'd been going to marry.

A second plan entered Hugh's head which was infinitely more satisfying. It would need patience, of course, but the end result would be worth the wait. He'd always liked a challenge, and let's face it, the highly complex woman sitting opposite him was a huge challenge.

He rose and moved to pull out the chair adjacent to him, then picked up her mug, saying, 'I'll get you a top-up. When I return I will explain my far from crazy proposal.'

He returned to find her frowning at him. 'You can't be serious, Hugh.'

He placed her refilled mug in front of her and sat back down. 'Naturally, I'm not proposing a normal marriage, or a public one. It would be a secret union in name only, to be discreetly dissolved at a later date. Of course, you'd have to sign a water-tight pre-nup, promising media silence and giving up any claim on my wealth. But you'd get the piece of paper you need to secure your friend's house. That is what you want, isn't it? What you value most in the world?'

'Yes, but…but…'

'But what?'

'What do *you* get out of this extraordinary and rather sacrificial gesture?'

Hugh smiled. 'Come, now, Kathryn, you of all people know I'm certainly not sacrificial. I'm selfish to the core. I get you, of course…staying on as my personal assistant,' he added, taking rueful note of the moment of shock which had flashed through her eyes.

He'd been right. She wouldn't have let him blackmail her into his bed. This way was much better all round. She would still be in his debt. She might even begin to like him a little.

Kathryn despised herself for that brief, perversely thrilling moment when she'd thought he meant something else. Then she despised *him*, for being what he said he was: selfish to the core.

What other man would marry his PA, simply to keep her working for him?

She eyed him quite coldly. 'Have you considered the possibility that I might still resign, once I take possession of Val's house?'

His face remained annoyingly confident. 'And do what? Sit around on your backside all day? I don't think so.'

'I could easily get another job up on the central coast.'

'Not with the kind of salary you're earning now. Or the excitement.'

'You think working for you is exciting?' she couldn't resist throwing at him.

His smile was wickedly sexy. 'Other girls would kill for your job.'

'You really are an incorrigibly arrogant man. I should say no to all of this. I know I should.'

'But you won't,' he said, still smiling.

'Why won't I?'

'Because you, Kathryn Hart, are an incorrigibly pragmatic woman. You know a good deal when you're offered it. Now, why don't you finish up your coffee and we'll take a drive up to Pearl Beach? I'd like to see this wonderful house for myself.'

'But we can't do that! At least, *I* can't. Do you have any idea how many emails and phone calls come through every day to your father's office which have to be answered?'

'Nothing *has* to be answered, Kathryn,' he pointed out with uncompromising logic. 'Nothing is so important that it can't wait. What would have happened if you hadn't come in today? Any normal girl would have called in sick. If you had, do you honestly think I would have sat around here all day, twiddling my thumbs? I'd have gone and played a game of golf. Now, no more objections. I'll inform Reception that you are unwell and I'm taking you home. It's not even a lie. You do look rather pale today. And from what you've told me, the house up at Pearl Beach is more your home than anywhere else.'

Kathryn stared across the table at him. She suspected she should say no to all these suggestions as well.

But she couldn't seem to find the willpower. She'd discovered last night that Hugh in masterful mode was a force not easily resisted…

Hugh saw the moment of surrender in her eyes and took ruthless advantage of it, not giving her time to revert to her usual stroppy self, making the necessary arrangements and steering her down to the basement car park in less than ten minutes.

The sigh she made when she settled into the passenger seat sounded weary, so he put on some soothing music and told her to just relax whilst he got them out of the city. She seemed only too happy to do so, even shutting her eyes after a while.

He didn't talk, focusing instead on getting across the bridge and into the right lane to carry them north. Despite having a car made for cruising, Hugh hadn't driven any great distance in ages and the recent road changes around North Sydney made for a few confusing moments, plus one rather abrupt lane change which sent her eyes flying open to glare over at him.

'Sorry,' he said swiftly. 'Haven't been up this way for ages. How long will it take us to get to Pearl Beach, by the way?'

'That depends. One and a half…two hours maybe?'

'And where is Pearl Beach exactly?' He'd never visited his friend's house up there, his mental picture of its location rather hazy. There were more beaches on the central coast than you could count.

'Do you know where Woy Woy is?'

'Yep. Been there. It's south of Gosford on the Brisbane water.'

'Pearl Beach is further south than that, past Umina.'

'Right.'

'You know, Val's house is really a very ordinary little house, not much more than a weekender. But it is right on the beach.'

'I presume it's empty,' Hugh said.

'Yes. The solicitor in charge of the estate didn't want to rent it out. Though he very kindly let me stay there for a few days over Christmas.'

'Mmm. Was Daryl with you?'

Kathryn wished he hadn't mentioned Daryl. She'd been trying not to think about him. Underneath, she was still in shock over his violent behaviour the previous night; plus there was her subsequent depressing realisation that their relationship hadn't been based on love at all.

So what had drawn them together in the first place? Why had she thought she loved him and vice versa?

The only answer Kathryn could come up with was sex, which was pretty pathetic. Maybe she wasn't capable of truly falling in love. Maybe she was as flawed in that regard as Hugh was.

'Well?' Hugh prompted. 'Was he or wasn't he?'

'Yes,' she said with a sigh.

She and Daryl had spent most of their time together arguing. By then Daryl had not been happy with her decision to never sell the house, once he'd seen it for himself. He simply hadn't understood her emotional attachment to the place and thought she was being stupid.

Kathryn shook her head at this last thought. She should have known back then that Daryl didn't really love her. If he had, he would have understood. And he would never, ever have hit her.

Her hand lifted to lightly touch the bruise on her cheek. It felt even sorer, and bigger. Truly, she must look a fright.

'Did the solicitor meet Daryl?' Hugh asked suddenly.

'What? No, no, he didn't.'

'That's lucky. Still, best he doesn't meet me, either.'

'But he'll see your name on the marriage certificate.'

'Parkinson is quite a common name. Does he know you work for me?'

'No, I've never mentioned it.'

'In that case we should be able to keep my true identity a secret.'

'But how? We'll have to have someone marry us. And there have to be witnesses. Even if we only go to the registry office, you'll be recognised.'

'I'll make sure I'm not.'

'How?'

'Amazing what a blond wig and sunglasses can achieve. I might get you a blonde wig as well. That way,' he said, flashing her a wicked grin, 'we'll both be incognito.'

Kathryn rolled her eyes at him. 'This is insane. You know that, don't you?'

'Come, now, Kathryn, stop taking life quite so seriously.'

'It's all very well for you. You're never serious about anything!'

'I've nothing to be serious about. And neither have you. Look on the bright side. Yesterday you were engaged to a jealous creep who would have made your life hell. Today you're free as a bird, to do as you please, with whomever you please.'

Kathryn wished he hadn't said that, wished he hadn't

glanced over at her right at that moment with those sexy blue eyes of his all a-twinkle and his sensually shaped lips curved back into a provocative smile.

An image immediately filled her mind, that of herself and Hugh together, not as they were at this moment, side by side in a car. But naked, in a bed.

Kathryn reefed her eyes away from his, terrified that he might be able to read her thoughts. The fact that she would be secretly wanting him to make love to her was shocking enough. But it would be much worse if he ever guessed.

'Only men like you are totally free to do as they please,' she snapped, 'with whomever they please.'

His laughter caused her to whip her eyes back round to glower at him.

'It's true,' she declared. 'When's the last time you had a lady of your choice knock you back?'

His smile was lopsided and rather wry. 'Not that long ago, actually.'

'I don't believe you.'

'It's true, nevertheless.'

Kathryn frowned, only then realising that the passing parade of females in Hugh's life had slowed down lately. Maybe he'd finally fancied a female with some common sense, someone who wanted more than just a temporary ride on the gravy train of Hugh's five-star life.

'I haven't give up hope yet, however,' he added.

I'll bet you haven't, she thought tartly, at the same time struggling to ignore the jolt of jealousy created by this confident announcement. The bitter truth was that not too many women could hold out indefinitely against Hugh's charm. Kathryn suspected this poor creature was already condemned to failure. Sooner or later, the girl would find herself in

Hugh's bed, a willing victim to his superbly practised brand of romance.

Such thinking made Kathryn realise she should be grateful that Hugh didn't fancy *her*. Because during the last two days she'd discovered she was no different from the rest of his conquests. She was just as silly, just as weak.

'The traffic's worse than I thought it would be at this time of day,' Hugh remarked.

'It's Friday,' she replied. 'Lots of people take a flexi-day on Friday, then head north for a long weekend of sun and surf. But, really, this traffic's not too bad. It'll be much worse this afternoon.'

'You sound like you've made this trip a lot.'

'I was brought up on the Central Coast. When I first starting working, I used to commute to Sydney by car every day. When it got to be a four-hour round trip I moved to the Big Smoke.'

'Four hours a day! God, what a waste of time. And of a life.'

'I agree, but some people have no alternative. Especially nowadays, with rental properties in Sydney being in short supply.'

'Yes, I was reading about that the other day. I've asked Russ to look around for some investment apartments for me.'

'Who's Russ?' Kathryn asked. She knew the names of several of Hugh's ex-girlfriends, but wasn't familiar with his male friends. Their photos didn't get into the glossies the way the women's did.

'Russell McClain of McClain Real Estate. He's one of my best friends. We went to school together.'

'Oh…' Another silver tail.

'Now, don't go jumping to incorrect conclusions, madam,' Hugh chided. 'Russ has worked extremely hard to get where he's got. He was a scholarship boy at school.'

'Lucky him.'

Kathryn felt herself on the end of a sharp glance. 'That was totally uncalled-for.'

She sighed. 'You're right. I'm sorry.'

'For what? For assuming that all my friends are like me? Lazy, spoiled and selfish?'

'I didn't say that.'

'But you thought it.'

Kathryn remained stiffly silent.

'I can't blame you if you think that of me,' he went on. 'But I won't have my friend tarred with the same brush. Russ is a great guy. Not only is he a very hard worker, but he's also honest, decent and loyal. You'd like him.'

Kathryn couldn't help but be impressed with Hugh's defence of his friend. He'd sounded pretty loyal himself just then.

'Is he one of the men you play golf with every Thursday?' she asked.

Kathryn had made a point of not asking Hugh much about his social life, experience having taught her to always keep her boss at a safe distance. Given the present circumstances, however, that seemed a bit silly.

'Yep,' he replied. 'Russ and Jimmy boy.'

'Who's Jimmy boy?'

'James Logan. Of Images fame. You must have heard of him.'

'Of course. Who hasn't?' Even if he hadn't been Sydney's most successful advertising man, his marriage to a super-model—and subsequent divorce—had given him some notoriety.

'I went to school with him as well. And no, James wasn't a scholarship boy. His father had made a fortune in transport. Not that his father bankrolled Images. He didn't. Jimmy boy built that business from scratch. I suspect he had something to prove to his old man. He's a bit on the intense side, is James. And somewhat ruthless when he wants to be.'

'Aren't most successful businessmen these days?'

'Some of us are.'

Kathryn refrained from commenting that she didn't categorise him as a successful businessman. He would inherit his fortune, not make it for himself. Still, he'd certainly impressed her yesterday with the way he'd handled that board meeting. He really was very intelligent, with brilliant people skills. It was a pity that he didn't have a better work ethic. Or, indeed, better ethics all round.

Still, she could not bring herself to think too badly of him today. No matter how selfish his motives, she would be eternally grateful to him for his offer of marriage.

'I don't think I've thanked you properly,' she said suddenly. 'You have no idea what it will mean to me, having Val's house in my life.'

'Which is why I want to see this place for myself. What time is it?'

Kathryn glanced at her wristwatch. 'Just after eleven.'

They finally made it to the motorway, the city quickly left behind as Hugh put his foot down.

'I could put the top down, if you like,' he said as they zoomed over the crest of a hill.

'I'd rather you didn't.' Kathryn was afraid she might like it too much. Or begin having even more fantasies about herself and Hugh.

'Fine,' he said in his usual easy-going fashion. 'So, is there anywhere decent to eat at Pearl Beach?'

'There's a very good restaurant right on the beach,' she told him. 'But it's often frequented by the rich and famous. So I don't think it's a good idea for you to take me there. Not if you want to keep our relationship a secret.'

'We don't have a relationship.'

'You know what I mean. I suggest we stop at Woy Woy on the way through and I'll get us a takeaway. Then we can eat it in Val's house.'

'But how will we get in? It'd be all locked up, surely.'

'I had copies of the key made at Christmas. There's only the one.'

His sidewards glance showed surprise. 'That was naughty of you.'

'I suppose it was. But at the time, I thought it would soon be mine.'

'And so it will be.'

'Yes,' she choked out.

'You're not going to cry again, are you?'

'Would it matter if I did?'

'Yes,' he said sharply.

'I don't see why.'

'I can't cope with women crying.'

'Then I suggest you treat them better.'

He laughed. 'Max was so right about you.'

'In what way?'

'He said it would do me good to have a woman around who didn't pander to me. Who always told me the truth.'

Kathryn stared over at him. Then she laughed. If only he knew…

He stared back at her for a second. 'Do you know, I think that's the first time I've heard you laugh out loud?'

'Is it really?'

'Yeah. I've heard the occasional snigger. But not a real laugh.'

'Oh, dear, you make me sound awful.'

'Not awful. Just way too serious. Life is very short. You don't want to look back on it and regret that you haven't lived it to its fullest.'

Kathryn wasn't sure what to make of that statement. It was rather facile, she thought. Especially coming from a man born with all the privileges money could bring. He had no idea what it was to live the life she'd lived as a child.

'Life is not always easy, Hugh,' she said, somewhat defensively. 'Sometimes, survival is the name of the game. You don't have a clue what it's like to wonder where your next meal is coming from. Or whether you'll be able to go on the simplest school excursion, because there isn't the money to pay for it.'

'No,' he returned slowly. 'No, I don't. But having an excess of money is not all it's cracked up to be. It doesn't solve all of life's problems. It creates problems of its own.'

'My heart bleeds for you.'

He laughed. 'My, but you're a sarcastic cow.'

'Yes, I know. It's one of my failings.'

'And the others are?'

'Being bossy and controlling. And wanting everything to be super-organised. I can't stand untidiness or a lack of planning.'

He laughed again. 'Tell me about it.'

'I've tried to. On many occasions.'

'With some success.'

'Oh, come, now,' she said drily. 'I *have* noticed a small improvement this past week. But, generally speaking, you're totally irresponsible and unreliable.'

'Really? That's good, then. There's nothing more boring than people who are responsible and reliable.'

'Are you saying I'm boring?'

'Not today you're not,' he countered with a breezy smile.

'You're here with me, aren't you? Playing hooky from work, and laughing and looking quite deliciously happy, if I may be so presumptuous to say so, Kat, darling.'

She sucked a breath in sharply. 'Don't call me that!'

His head turned her way and their eyes met. 'Don't be silly,' he said, his eyes caressing hers in the most incredibly seductive fashion. 'Kat suits you admirably. Or was it the 'darling' that offended you? Yes, of course it was,' he added before returning his eyes to the road. 'Sorry. I don't mean anything by it. I call all my women friends darling.'

'But I'm not your woman friend,' she protested, her face feeling hot all of a sudden. 'I'm your PA!'

'And soon-to-be wife.'

'Not a real wife.'

'I suppose not. But that doesn't stop us being friends, does it? I feel more like a friend to you today than a boss. And I never call my friends by their full names. So from now on, I'm going to call you Kat whether you like it or not.'

'You really are impossible!'

'So I've been told on many occasions. Now, where are we exactly? You might have made this trip a thousand times, but I haven't been up this way for yonks and I haven't been concentrating. I know we passed over the Hawkesbury River a little while back. How long before I get off the freeway?'

'Not for another ten minutes or so. We have to go over the Mooney Mooney bridge first. Then you take the Gosford exit. After that, I'll tell you where to go.'

He glanced over at her and grinned. 'I'll bet you will.'

CHAPTER EIGHT

PEARL BEACH was extremely pretty but rather remote, surrounded by bushland and with only one road leading into it. There were more houses than Hugh had anticipated; most were within walking distance of the beach and lots more were built on the side of a hill which faced north and provided splendid views of the ocean and the village below.

The wonder house sat at the northern end of the beach, on flat land, the front facing away from the sea, the back garden less than twenty metres from the sand.

Kathryn hadn't exaggerated when she'd said it was an ordinary little house. It certainly was. But the simple weatherboard façade had charm, with symmetrically placed windows on either side of a sweet front door—painted a bright blue—and a wide, wrap-around verandah which had an assortment of battered seating that obviously wasn't considered good enough to steal. There was no garden to speak of, just the odd bush or two, and a lawn which had given up the ghost years before, perhaps because the ground was mostly sand.

After a very brief trip to the bathroom, Hugh declined a more extensive tour inside in favour of sitting down on the back verandah in an ancient cane chair and tucking into his hamburger; its mouth-watering smell had been tantalising him since their stop in Woy Woy, a short time earlier.

'This is the best burger I've ever had,' Hugh said in muffled tones as he munched in.

'Watch that the beetroot doesn't drip on your trousers,' Kathryn advised sharply.

He quickly parted his legs to avoid just that, then glanced over at where she was standing on the verandah, looking out at the water. 'Aren't you hungry?' he asked between swallows.

'I'll eat soon.'

He watched her put her own paper-wrapped burger on a small and rather rusty iron table, then settle herself into a faded old swing seat, her ankles crossing underneath her as she gently rocked back and forth.

Her sigh wasn't a weary one this time, it carried contentment.

Hugh stared at the transformation in her face, noting the softening in her eyes and around her mouth. Her body was more relaxed too—less tension in her shoulders.

She wasn't wearing that killer black suit today. She was dressed in a very conservative grey number, the outfit lifted from sombre to subtly sexy by a pale pink silk blouse. She'd taken her jacket off when they'd climbed out of the car at Woy Woy, the temperature outside having reached thirty-two degrees. He'd dispensed with his own jacket and tie at that stage.

Hugh had always liked pink on a woman. And silk. The combination would have done things to him even if it hadn't been worn by a woman whom he would have desired in sackcloth and ashes.

His eyes kept returning to her as he ate. Hopefully they were unreadable, because every time he looked at her these days his mind soon filled with erotic thoughts. At the moment, he was picturing her sitting in that swing with nothing on except that blouse, her naked nipples outlined in pink silk. In his fantasy he imagined that the softness in her face was caused by hours of lovemaking, all the tension in her body totally erased. In his daydream, she'd wanted him over and over. Soon, she would want him again. Soon, she'd look at him and the urgency would be back in her eyes.

Her head turned and their eyes met over the last bite of his hamburger.

Kathryn reefed her eyes away from his, embarrassed to find him watching her.

He must think I'm mad. Sitting here, not eating.

She rose and went over to where she'd left the food, quickly sliding the cardboard box out of the bag, then carefully lifting the over-stuffed hamburger to her lips. It was, indeed, very tasty. But the various juices, plus the tomato sauce, did make it difficult not to make a mess. She hurried over to the edge of the verandah and leant slightly forward, making sure any drips didn't get on her own clothes.

She didn't glance his way but she was aware of his eyes on her the whole time, making her self-conscious, not only because she was eating, but also of her whole body. She wished he would say something, but he didn't. She ate more quickly, demolishing the hamburger in record time, then, because she didn't have a serviette, started licking her sticky fingers, one by one.

Hugh almost groaned out loud. Hell, he couldn't take much more of this.

'I'm going inside to wash up,' he said.

The bathroom was straight out of the ark. So was the rest of the house. But, for some strange reason, he still liked it.

'The bathroom and kitchen could do with some modernising,' he said when he emerged back out onto the verandah to thankfully find her finished with the finger-licking. 'But you're right. There is a feel-good feel about this place. It would be a shame to knock it down.'

She looked at him in utter surprise. 'You really mean that?'

'Yes, of course. I wouldn't say it if I didn't mean it.'

'I can't tell you how much I love it here,' she said.

'You don't have to tell me. I can see that, too.'

She gave him a thoughtful look. 'You do have a sensitive side, don't you?'

He smiled a wry smile. 'So my friends tell me.'

'But you don't think so?'

Hugh shrugged. 'I am what I am.'

'Which is?'

His smile widened. 'Arrogant, irresponsible, unreliable. Oh, and selfish to the core.'

Her head tipped charmingly to one side. 'I'm not so sure that you are. Selfish, that is. If you were, you wouldn't be prepared to do what you're going to do for me. I don't believe you'd go to the trouble of marrying me, just to keep me on as your PA. That's ridiculous. You just said that to hide the true reason behind your offer.'

'And the true reason is?' Hugh asked, feeling half guilty, half amused.

'Deep down, you're kind.'

He couldn't help it. He laughed. And then, when her face flushed with an embarrassed confusion, he compounded his stupidity by doing the one thing he'd warned himself not to do.

He pulled her into his arms and kissed her.

CHAPTER NINE

IF ONLY she'd pulled back and slapped his face straight away.

But she didn't. There was a second or two of frozen shock but then her mouth melted beneath his.

Her lips fell wantonly apart, allowing his tongue easy entry. By the time she did struggle out of his embrace it was way too late. The smouldering fire of his passion for her had burst into flame and his conscience was well and truly routed.

'What on earth do you think you're doing?' she gasped, her eyes wide, the back of her hand lifting to press against her mouth.

'Showing you the real reason behind my offer of marriage.'

She just stared at him.

'As unlikely as it might seem, Kat, darling,' he said with a wry little smile, 'I want you, the way men have been wanting women since Adam and Eve.'

'I don't believe you!' she blurted out.

'Shall I show you again?'

She took a shaky step backwards.

Hugh slid his hands in his trouser pockets for safe keeping.

'I'm not sure how it happened,' he went on, having decided that the unvarnished truth was the only road to success at this stage. That, and her obsession with this house. 'I didn't hire you initially because I fancied you. I'm not stupid enough to do something like that. This unwanted…attraction…crept up on me. By the time I became aware of it, you were engaged to Daryl. Whether you believe me or not, I do not tamper with engaged—or married—women. Though heaven knows, I've been tempted. When you announced this morning that your marriage was off I couldn't have been happier. At last, I thought. But then you said you were going to resign.' He gave her a look which carried considerable frustration. 'That was the straw that broke this camel's back!'

Kathryn could not believe what she was hearing. She did not know whether she felt flattered, or furious.

'So you offered to marry me, not because you wanted me to have this house, but because you wanted to…to have sex with me?'

'Ultimately.'

That was the part she couldn't get her head around. That he fancied her like that. Why her? She wasn't anything special. 'But you said it was to be a marriage in name only.'

He shrugged. 'I didn't think you'd go for anything else to begin with. I was playing for time.'

Playing for time. And playing with her. And there she'd been, thinking he was sensitive. And kind!

'You planned to seduce me,' she said, her voice incredulous but her heart thumping madly behind her ribs.

'I'm not keen on the word seduction. I hoped to persuade you into my bed.'

'My God…' Why, oh, why did she have to find his actions so exciting? She should have been tearing strips off him. Instead, wildly erotic thoughts were running around in her head, rendering her temporarily speechless.

'I take it you don't like the idea,' he stated flatly. 'In that case let me put it to you another way: if you still want this house, I suggest you start liking the idea.'

'That's blackmail!'

'I prefer to call it negotiation.'

Kathryn hoped that her underlying excitement came over as anger. 'So you won't marry me now, unless I let you have sex with me.'

'I wouldn't put it quite that crudely. But yes, that's the bottom line.'

'For how long?'

His eyebrows arched. 'Are we referring to individual acts here, or the length of our sexual relationship?'

Now she *was* angry. 'Stop trying to be funny. I don't find this funny at all. It's humiliating and demeaning.'

He looked genuinely surprised. 'I don't see why. You went to bed with Daryl, a man you didn't love. You were even prepared to marry him, just to get this house. Now, that would have been humiliating and demeaning.'

'It wasn't like that and you know it.'

'Actually, no, I don't know it. If you're honest, Kat, darling, you'll see I'm telling the truth.'

'Don't keep calling me that ridiculous name.'

'Methinks she doth protest too much.'

'And what does that mean?'

'It means that you betrayed yourself a little while ago when I kissed you.' Taking his hands out of his pockets he walked slowly towards her. 'You responded for a few seconds, Kat, darling,' he said as he lifted a gentle hand to her cheek, the one without the bruise. 'You liked my mouth on yours. You *liked* it,' he repeated, his eyes locking onto hers.

Pride demanded she not surrender to the feelings which his touch was evoking. But, oh…she wanted to. Wanted to say, yes, yes, I liked your mouth on mine. And, yes, I'd happily go to bed with you, with or without a certificate of marriage.

Somehow, she managed to keep her eyes steady and her heartbeat from totally going off the planet. 'You're a good kisser,' she said with superbly feigned composure.

'I'm an even better lover,' he told her.

What an ego he had!

'And who told you that?' she threw at him. 'Surely you haven't been believing the gold-diggers you've been dating. Women like that tell men like you whatever they want to hear.'

For a split second his eyes darkened, but then they cleared, and he smiled.

'Then I suggest you follow their lead. You're the one who wants this house, and I don't think you're going to get another man to marry you at this late stage.'

'You really are a wicked devil.'

'You can always say no.'

'I could.'

'But you won't.'

'No,' she said slowly, doing her best to remain calm. 'I won't.'

'Shall we seal the deal with a kiss?'

He didn't wait for her to answer, just gripped her shoulders with firm hands and lowered his mouth to hers.

She held her breath, willing herself not to move, not to part her lips, not to give him any more satisfaction.

She might have succeeded if he'd been rough. But he wasn't. His mouth was gentle, his lips brushing lightly over hers, back and forth, back and forth. When he started running his tongue-tip over them, Kathryn knew she was lost.

When she moaned and opened her mouth, Hugh experienced a rush of dark pleasure unlike anything he'd ever felt before.

He hadn't wanted to blackmail her into his bed. Hadn't

wanted to take such a ruthless line of action. But, damn it all, it was exciting. *She* was exciting.

Because she wasn't faking it. He could tell. She didn't *want* to enjoy his kisses, didn't *want* to respond. But she did, nevertheless. And now there was no going back, for either of them.

His tongue drove in deep, his arms sweeping down around her bottom so that he could pull her hard against him and show her how much he wanted her.

She groaned and struggled against him. But he held her fast, held her and kissed her till she dissolved against him one more time, sliding her arms up around his neck and showing him that she was his, in the only way he cared about.

It was at that precise point that Hugh lifted his mouth, removed her arms from his neck and took a step backwards. Her wildly dilated eyes were immensely satisfying; so was their glazed expression—not quite adoring yet, but he was hopeful.

'I think,' he said, doing his level best to ignore his extremely painful erection, 'that we should postpone this till we are somewhere more suitable. And more private,' he added, nodding towards the nearby beach, where several groups of people were enjoying the hot weather as only Australians could.

He had to admire the speed with which she gathered herself.

'If you think I'm going to sleep with you before we're married, Hugh Parkinson,' she said sharply, 'then you can think again.'

Hugh toyed with the idea of taking her right then and there, but decided that having to wait a while would multiply his pleasure a thousandfold. Not five weeks, though, that was ridiculous.

'In that case, I'll organise a special licence.' He'd organised one for Russ to get married before Christmas. There was no reason why he couldn't do the same for himself. Money opened all doors. He didn't even need a legitimate excuse. 'We'll be man and wife before the week is out.'

Kathryn's mouth dropped open, then snapped shut again.

She still couldn't get used to Hugh wanting to sleep with her this much.

Why? What was it about her which was making him go to such ridiculous lengths to have her? She wasn't beautiful. Neither did she have a great body, having an inclination to put on weight easily. Daryl had commented early on in their relationship that she could do with losing a few pounds, which was why she'd started going to the gym. Not with any great success so far. She was still way too hippy, and with far too much bottom. Her breasts were OK, she supposed, but they needed good support to look their best. All in all, she couldn't compare to the stunning-looking women who'd regularly graced Hugh's arm in the past.

Hugh had admitted that he hadn't been instantly smitten with her. Kathryn could only imagine that she'd become some kind of perverse challenge; that she'd sparked his interest because she'd shown none of her own.

It was all very confusing. But perversely flattering too. She would have to watch herself. The last thing she wanted was to stupidly fall in love with him.

'I'm not going to live with you,' she said sharply.

'Fine.'

'And I'll be filing for divorce as soon as I take possession of this house. I still have plans to have a family, you know. And I'm not getting any younger.'

'Fine.'

'I'll be resigning then, as well. You do realise that.'

'Yes,' he said without turning a hair.

He doesn't care about me at all, she suddenly realised. Either as a person, or his PA. He just wants to screw me silly, then send me on my merry way.

His ruthlessness should have appalled her. It *did* appall her. But it turned her on at the same time.

'Till that happens, however,' he added, his eyes quite hard as they held hers, 'I expect you not to reject me sexually.'

Kathryn's head spun at his coolly delivered demand.

What on earth was she getting into here?

'I won't be a party to anything kinky,' she said, then wished she hadn't. Did sex on his desk count as kinky?

'I give you my word that I won't expect you to do anything you don't like.'

Kathryn didn't feel all that comforted by this assurance. She suspected that she might like just about anything with this wicked devil of a man.

'So where are we going to get married?' she went on in a desperate attempt to get her mind off the subject of sex. 'Still the registry office?'

'No, I've changed my mind about that. I have a minister friend who won't say a word to the Press, and who won't ask any awkward questions. We'll have a private little ceremony at my place, with my golfing buddies as witnesses. They won't breathe a word to anyone, either.'

'But surely they'll ask questions?'

'Undoubtedly,' he said rather drily.

'What will you tell them?'

'The truth. To a degree. I'll leave out the sex part. They'll think I'm mad.'

'You *are* mad.'

His smile was wry. 'We're both mad. You, about this house. And me…about you.'

Kathryn still could not come to terms with his confessed desire for her. It seemed…unbelievable. But if it got her Val's house, then she couldn't regret the fact that she'd somehow piqued Hugh's interest. Coming here today had reaffirmed what this place meant to her. Without it, she'd be lost. She'd have done practically anything to get it. Hugh was right. She wouldn't have said yes to Daryl's proposal if marriage to him hadn't secured Val's house for her.

It was why she was saying yes to Hugh's much less conventional proposal.

That *was* the only reason, wasn't it, Kathryn? she asked herself as she glanced over at his handsome face.

His eyebrows suddenly drew together into a frown. 'What is it?' he asked. 'What's wrong?'

Kathryn did her best to clear whatever it was he'd seen in her face. 'I was just thinking,' she said, valiantly ignoring the panic which her thoughts had produced.

'About what?'

'Practicalities.'

He sighed. 'I should have been expecting this, I suppose. And what practicalities would that be?'

'Birth control, for starters.'

'You want me to use protection.'

Did she? 'Well, I…um…I am on the Pill. And I made Daryl get checked out when we got engaged. He was clear, but…'

'Don't worry. I never rely on the Pill. I'll come well-prepared.'

Kathryn winced at his rather evocative turn of phrase. She shouldn't have started this conversation right now. It made her think about having sex with him again, though this time not on a desk, but in a bed—all night long.

'You'll have to organise that pre-nup for me to sign this

week,' she swept on, annoyed at her one-track mind. 'How are you going to do that without more people finding out we're getting married?'

'Our family lawyer spends half his life writing up pre-nups. Henry won't say a word to anyone, if I ask him not to. He's paid extremely well to keep the Parkinson family's secrets. Anything else, Kat, darling?'

'Yes,' she snapped. 'There will be no more Kat, darlings. Not only does it sound ridiculous, but it's also a dead giveaway. You've always called me Kathryn. Please keep doing so.'

His sigh sounded resigned. 'Very well…Kathryn. Is that it for the practicalities?'

'I can't think of anything else right now.' She'd have to cancel all her previous wedding arrangements. She'd start making phone calls as soon as she got back to Sydney. The thought was not only dismaying but also slightly shocking. Yesterday, she'd been all set to marry Daryl. It seemed in-credible that, less than twenty-four hours later, she was planning a very different type of marriage to a very different type of man.

She stared over at Hugh, who was leaning against the verandah railing with his hands deep in his trouser pockets, his handsome face turned away from hers towards the sea.

Impossible to look at him now without being besieged by a host of confusing emotions. As much as she felt she should dislike and despise him for blackmailing her into his bed like this, she could not seem to do so. Kathryn supposed it was a common feminine failing to be immensely flattered when a man admitted to an all-consuming passion. She'd had men declare that they fancied her like mad before this, but never a man like Hugh, who could have his pick of all the women in Australia, maybe even the world.

His desire for her was not only flattering, but also incredibly seductive. It made her feel…weak.

Of course, sex had always been a weakness with her. She loved everything to do with lovemaking. Loved the way it could take her away from the sometimes harsh reality of life into a world where nothing existed but the pleasure of the moment.

Hugh, she imagined, might just leave her previous experiences in the shade.

He suddenly turned his head to face her.

'I think we should be getting back to Sydney,' he said abruptly. 'Otherwise we'll catch the peak-hour traffic going through the city.'

'Are we going back to the office?'

He glanced at his watch. 'No. I'll drive you straight home. But I'll still go over the bridge then onto the western distributor. Come on, let's go.'

'I have to lock up first.'

'I'll wait for you in the car.'

Kathryn took several deep breaths as she walked through the house one last time, checking the windows and trying to absorb the peaceful atmosphere which she'd experienced out on the verandah earlier, but which seemed to be eluding her now.

Her nerves had become jangled, of course. Hugh had jangled them, with his passionate kisses, his provocative admissions and his plans for a much quicker marriage. If he could organise a special licence—and Kathryn had no doubt he would—she would soon be his legal wife.

It was a mind-boggling thought.

'I won't think about that now,' she said, then smiled when she realised she'd said exactly what Scarlet said in *Gone with the Wind*. Kathryn didn't add that she'd think about it tomorrow. Because she knew she'd think about it again tonight. All night, probably.

'I'll be back,' she promised the house as she turned the lock on the front door. 'And next time, I'll be alone.'

CHAPTER TEN

HUGH wasn't on the road very long before he began to regret not seducing Kathryn when they'd been up at Pearl Beach. He really should have swept her off to bed whilst he had the chance. The unexpectedly vulnerable woman she'd become after his kisses on the verandah was no longer to be seen. She'd well and truly disappeared, replaced by the extremely practical and irritatingly pragmatic creature he'd hired.

'By the way,' she'd said when first returning to his car, 'you'll need birth certificates to get any type of marriage licence. Mine's at home, in my dressing-table drawer. I'll get it for you when you drop me off. Oh, and please don't go buying wedding rings. Some intuitive salesperson might alert the media. We can use the rings I bought for my marriage to Daryl. I did pay for them after all. And it's not as though we'll be wearing them afterwards.'

Her coolly composed demeanour did what it always did to him—made him want her all the more. It was just as well he'd moved their marriage forward. As it was, a week would seem like an eternity. His imagining that the wait might increase his physical pleasure did not compute at this precise moment. He was literally in pain, his flesh aching with need, his mind in a lather of frustration.

In desperation he put on the radio, thereby stopping any further conversation. She settled to staring out of the passenger window, leaving Hugh to wonder and worry what she might be thinking.

She was a mystery all right. Normally, he didn't have any trouble reading women. Their behaviour towards him was quite transparent. Kathryn was an enigma. Clearly, she wasn't harbouring any secret passion for him. At the same time, she didn't seem overly bothered by the prospect of going to bed with him. She'd enjoyed his kisses.

But not as much as he'd enjoyed kissing her.

That had been a mistake on his part, kissing her. You didn't give a man dying of thirst a tiny sip of water, then snatch the rest of it away without expecting him to go crazy.

Hugh felt as if he was going crazy at that moment. His reaching Ashfield could not come soon enough. He wouldn't walk her to the door. He'd wait in the car till she got her birth certificate, then he would be off and away from temptation.

Hopefully, by the time he had to face her again the following Monday, he'd have himself firmly under control.

Meanwhile, the drive down the motorway back to Sydney seemed endless. Half an hour later they reached the edges of the city, then, after another forty frustrating minutes of negotiating Friday-afternoon traffic, Hugh turned into Kathryn's street in Ashfield.

The clock on the dashboard showed five past four as he eased the Ferrari into the kerb outside her block of flats.

'Wait here,' she said as she immediately opened the passenger door and started getting out, her jacket and handbag in her hands. 'I won't be long.'

Her sinking back down into the seat startled him, so did her distressed groan.

'What is it?' he asked a bit sharply.

'That car over there,' she said, pointing to a dark blue Falcon parked in a guest bay at the front of the building. 'That's Daryl's car.'

Maybe if Hugh were in a calmer frame of mind, he'd have been able to control the surge of violent anger which washed through him. As it was, he didn't even try.

'Good,' he bit out. 'Save me having to go find the bastard for myself.'

Kathryn's head whipped round, alarm on her face. 'You're not going to do anything silly, are you? I mean…Daryl was brought up in a very tough neighbourhood.'

He had to smile. 'Don't you worry about me. I can handle myself. Come on, let's go see what he's up to.'

Even before she led Hugh up the stairs to her first-floor flat, Kathryn felt sick with apprehension. If Daryl was there, he wasn't going to appreciate her being with Hugh. Things were sure to turn very nasty indeed.

Daryl was standing on the landing, spray-painting something onto the door. He whirled when he heard footsteps behind him, his eyes showing surprise at seeing Kathryn at this hour of the day. When he saw Hugh behind her, however, his surprise quickly turned to guilt.

Kathryn soon saw why: the word SLUT had been painted in bold red letters on the wood-grained door.

Kathryn watched, wide-eyed, as Hugh pushed past her and advanced on Daryl, grabbing him by his shirt collar, pressing him back against the wall and hauling him up onto his toes so that they were eye to eye.

'If I ever see your ugly face anywhere near Kathryn again,' Hugh said in a voice which was chillingly cold, 'I'll have you arrested for assault. And libel,' he added, nodding towards the door. 'Don't even begin to imagine that you'll get off. I'm a very wealthy man and I have one hell of a lot of contacts in the legal profession. Do I make myself clear?'

Daryl nodded with astonishing meekness.

'I would also suggest you find yourself another job, in another city, in another state. You're no longer welcome in this town. Now, I'll just see you to your car,' he ground out, and started pushing Daryl towards the staircase, one hand cupped at the back of Daryl's neck, the other firmly on his shoulder. 'Wouldn't want you falling down and hurting yourself. I'll be back shortly, Kathryn,' he threw over his shoulder at her. 'Go inside and put on the kettle.'

Kathryn didn't go inside. She just stood there, staring rather blankly after Hugh, her mind still dazed by what had just happened. There she'd been, worrying about Daryl's temper, worrying about what he might do to Hugh.

That worry had been totally misplaced. Hugh had been right when he'd said he could handle himself. He certainly could.

Kathryn had never had *any* man stand up for her the way Hugh had just done. Really, he'd been quite magnificent.

He'd made her feel almost…loved.

'What are you doing, still standing out here?'

She whirled at his sudden return, shocked at the way just the sight of him made her heart pound.

Not with love, Kathryn realised ruefully, but with excitement…sexual excitement.

She flushed as she glanced at the word on her door.

Maybe I *am* a slut, she thought. I must be if I'm wanting Hugh this much so soon after breaking up with Daryl.

'Don't let what that creep did upset you,' Hugh said. 'He's gone now and he won't be coming back. Trust me.'

Her eyes slowly returned to his. 'Yes. Thank you, Hugh. For everything. You were quite…wonderful.'

He didn't say a word. Just stood there, staring deep into her eyes. His expression was unreadable but his body language reeked of the same sexual tension which had her insides in an excruciating knot. Kathryn knew that if she allowed herself to move, she would literally throw herself into his arms.

'It's no use,' he muttered at last.

'What's no use?' she asked way too breathlessly.

'I can't possibly wait a week. I can't wait another single night. I have reached the point of no return, Kathryn. I have to have you. Please don't say no.'

Her heartbeat, which had become suspended, lurched back into a wildly galloping rhythm. For a split second she was tempted to tell him that she felt the same way about him. But something—some well-honed survival instinct—warned her not to give him that much power over her. Better he think she was agreeing out of gratitude, or greed.

'All right,' she choked out. 'But…'

'But what?' he snapped, exasperation in his voice.

'Not here.'

'Hell, no,' he said. 'We'll go to my place. Now hurry inside and get that birth certificate. And anything else you might need for a sleepover.'

'I'm staying the night?'

'What do you think?'

'I think I'm staying the night.'

'Good thinking. Now, no more conversation, please, especially in the car. Or I'll probably run into the back of a truck.'

CHAPTER ELEVEN

HUGH'S apartment block came as a surprise to Kathryn. Firstly, it was a rather ordinary-looking building, about five or six storeys high. Secondly, there was little security to speak of, although he did use a plastic key-card to get into the underground car park. Not quite where you would expect a billionaire's son and heir to live. Still, it did overlook Bondi Beach and, inside, it was probably very luxurious.

Hugh parked his Ferrari in one of the two spaces allotted to apartment number twelve, then he escorted a—by then—extremely tense Kathryn to the lift.

'You can talk now,' he said with a wry smile her way. 'We're safely here.'

'I'm not sure I want to talk,' she replied somewhat stiffly. How could she possibly chatter when all she could think about was what they were about to do?

'That's fine by me,' he said in gravelly tones, and pressed the button on the third floor.

That surprised her too. She'd been thinking he probably lived in the penthouse.

'How about kissing?' he asked after the lift doors closed and the lift began to move. 'No, don't answer that. I don't really want to be compelled to ravage you in this lift. I want to take my time. And I want you naked.'

Kathryn's hand tightened around her carry-all. Dear heaven…

The lift stopped smoothly on the third floor, the doors opening with a soft, swooshing sound.

'This way,' he said, and led her down a plushly carpeted corridor to a door with the number twelve on it.

His apartment was spacious without being excessively large, the living room filled with an assortment of furniture and an eclectic mix of expensive *objets d'art*. The floor was polished timber, with an assortment of colourful rugs. The effect was warm and inviting, unlike his father's designer-decorated but extremely cold-looking penthouse.

'This way,' he directed again, and taking her hand, drew her down a side hallway into a bedroom which *was* huge… and utterly devoted to a billionaire bachelor's pleasure: shag-pile carpet underfoot, a king-sized bed and a plasma television built into the wall opposite the bed. On either side of the TV, sliding glass doors opened up out onto a wide balcony with the most breathtaking view of Bondi Beach. A doorway in the middle of a side wall gave Kathryn glimpses of a spacious *en suite* bathroom with a corner spa bath.

'Do you want to use the bathroom?' he asked her.

She nodded.

'I do too,' he told her. 'I'll duck down to the main bathroom. See you shortly.'

This interlude presented Kathryn with the opportunity for a reality check. Or it would have, if this whole scenario had felt real.

But it didn't.

'What is it he sees in me?' she asked her reflection in the bathroom mirror.

Kathryn knew that physically she couldn't compare with the kind of woman Hugh usually dated and obviously slept with: actresses and models, mostly, all of whom possessed outstanding beauty and figures which looked just as good without clothes.

A shudder ran through her as she thought of the moment when Hugh discovered that his PA's naked body wasn't going to live up to whatever fantasy had been playing in his mind.

'What are you doing in there?' he called through the door. 'Not taking your clothes off, I hope. I want to do that.' The door opened abruptly and Hugh walked in.

She was just standing there, looking at herself in the mirror. Looking unsure and, yes, nervous.

Hugh ignored the jab to his conscience. It was too late for guilt. Too late for anything but the inevitable.

She turned at his entry, her expression changing from nervousness to curiosity.

'Why me?' she asked him.

He smiled and reached up to begin doing what he'd dreamt of doing for months.

'Because of this,' he murmured as he removed first one hairpin, then another, then another, savouring the rush of dark pleasure as he watched her thick brown hair tumble down around her shoulders.

'And this,' he went on, his hands dropping to the buttons on her pink blouse.

'I...I still don't understand,' she said, her voice shaky, her eyes wide.

'Don't even try, babe,' he murmured. 'Can I at least call

you that? Of course I can. There's no one else to hear. You don't mind my talking, do you? I like to talk during sex.'

Finally the last button was undone, Hugh's heart skipping a beat as he peeled the blouse back off her shoulders. He let it flutter to the bathroom floor before sliding his hands back up her arms and over her softly rounded shoulders.

The bra she was wearing was white, but not in any way virginal. It was a silky, low-cut number, structured to enhance any female's bustline by pushing her breasts up and inwards, creating a cleavage on even the most small-breasted woman.

Kathryn had full, lush breasts which, in that bra, formed highly curved mounds of pale flesh, practically bursting from their confines.

'This is a very sexy bra,' he said, his fingers tracing the edges of the cups till they reached the front fastening. 'But your breasts don't need any enhancing.'

His knuckles showed white as he slowly unhooked the bra from her body then threw it away, his heart thundering behind his ribs. This was what he'd wanted to do for so long. This was what he'd craved seeing and feeling.

Adrenaline raced through his veins as his gaze focused on her naked breasts, which had settled into a lower and far more natural shape. No silicone there, Hugh thought excitedly, having grown sick and tired of being with women whose seemingly perfect breasts stayed in the same position, no matter what.

'So beautiful,' he said with a deep sigh of satisfaction as his hands lifted to cup them, then squeeze them, his thumbs rubbing over her deliciously large nipples at the same time.

Her gasp brought his eyes back up to her face.

'If you tell me you don't like that, then I won't believe you,' he chided softly.

'I...I...'

Her stammering delighted him, as did the slightly wild look in her eyes. Hugh knew sexual arousal when he saw it and felt it.

'It seems you won't have to just lie back and think of that silly little house after all,' he murmured as he continued to play with her already fiercely erect nipples. 'Do tell me if you want me to stop, beautiful. Or to move on...'

She seemed incapable of speaking, however, a response which appealed to Hugh's dark side. This was, after all, what he'd fantasised over, reducing his normally capable and irritatingly vocal assistant to a state of mindless sexual excitement which didn't allow thought, let alone speech; stripping her, not just of her clothes, but also of her ability to cut him down to size with some withering comment.

She moaned when he abandoned her breasts to undo the button on her waistband, her dilated pupils betraying that she was turned on to the max.

Hugh suddenly felt perversely calm. She was his now, to do with as he pleased. And he was pleased to do one hell of a lot!

Kathryn made no protest when he stripped her of the rest of her clothes. The time for protesting was long gone.

He swept her up into his arms, his clothed state making her even more brutally aware that she was totally naked before him. Naked in more ways than one.

She'd seen the triumph in his eyes when he'd rendered her speechless. Heard the satisfaction in his voice.

She should have felt humiliated. Should have raked up enough pride to say something back!

But she hadn't. And somehow none of that seemed to

matter. All that mattered was that he kept on making love to her and kept on telling her she was beautiful.

He laid her down on top of his bed, the silky blue quilt cool against her hot skin. She stared up at him, wanting to know what he was thinking, what he was feeling. But his face remained unreadable as he ran his hands lightly down her body, his hooded eyes following them.

'I love it that you're not skinny,' he said softly. When his fingers slid into her, she instinctively stiffened, not in protest, but in anticipation of what she was about to feel and what he was about to discover.

'So wet,' he whispered.

Kathryn tried not to react to his knowing touch, a futile and rather foolish gesture at this stage, and one which she swiftly abandoned, squirming with pleasure as his exploration became more intimate.

Dear God, she was going to come. Any second now.

'Not yet, beautiful,' he growled, and abruptly withdrew his hand. 'And not like that.'

When he stood up and began stripping, Kathryn was unable to take her eyes off him. He was the one who was beautiful, more beautiful than any man she'd ever been with; tall and broad-shouldered with a magnificently defined male body and the kind of smoothly silky olive skin which would be a joy to touch.

All his clothes were disposed of with incredible speed, Kathryn having little time to ogle more of his magnificence before he rejoined her on the bed.

'At last,' he muttered as he cupped her face then kissed her, a long, hot, hungry kiss which drove all thought from her head. When he pried her legs open with one of his knees and moved between them, she was more than ready for him.

'Damn and blast,' he muttered. 'You keep doing this to me.'

She stared up at him with blank eyes. 'Doing what?'

He just shook his head. 'I almost forgot the condom. Won't be a sec.'

She squeezed her eyes tightly shut, shocked at how tempted she was to tell him to just forget it. Not that he would. Hugh was no fool.

And if she had any common sense left in her—which was debatable—she wouldn't want him to have unprotected sex with her, either. The Pill was not one hundred per cent safe. Neither were condoms. But the two together had to be pretty foolproof.

'Surely you're not one of those women who likes to have sex with the lights out.'

Her eyes fluttered open to see him climb back onto the bed, her breath catching at the sight of his erection.

He rolled between her legs once more, his upper half propped up on his elbows.

'That's better,' he said, and reached up to smooth her hair back from her forehead. 'I want to see your eyes. Now...'

When his hand dropped down between their bodies, Kathryn automatically tensed. But he didn't put himself inside her straight away. Instead, he rubbed the smooth head of his manhood up and down between her legs till her already electrified nerve-endings felt they were going to explode. He watched her all the while, no doubt reading the urgency which her eyes had to be betraying.

'Hugh,' she choked out at last.

'Yes, beautiful?'

'Please...'

'You want me inside you.'

'Yes, yes,' she said, desperate now.

He took his time, filling her slowly, making her moan at

the feel of their flesh becoming one. Nothing, in all her life, had ever felt this good.

'Put your legs around me,' he ordered thickly.

When she did, he slid his hands under her bottom and held her hard against him.

'Put your arms around my neck. Yes, that's the way.' He smiled down at her. 'Tell me you like me just a little.'

She could not stop herself smiling back at him.

'Maybe a little,' she admitted.

'We're going to have a great time together.'

'Are we?'

'Absolutely.'

A horrible thought suddenly occurred to her. 'You…you will still marry me, won't you?'

His face showed mock-offence. 'Would I do that to you?'

'I have no idea what you'd do to me. I've never been with someone like you before.'

'Meaning?'

'I can't believe we're even having this conversation. I mean, what kind of man stops and chats at a time like this?'

He laughed. 'A man who doesn't have to feel guilty any more. But I *can* move and talk. Trust me.'

When he set up a slow, voluptuous rhythm with his hips, a wave of heat washed through her, her flesh clenching and unclenching around his.

He groaned the most sexy-sounding groan.

'Oh, babe, you're even better than I thought you'd be. That feels fantastic.'

'You feel pretty fantastic yourself,' she choked out.

'See? You can talk and move as well.'

'I…I think I'm going to come.'

'So soon?'

'Sorry.'

'Don't be. I'm not far behind you. But you first. I want to watch.'

His words sent her face flaming and her head spinning. But nothing short of death was going to stop her climaxing.

He didn't watch for long. At the moment her first spasm struck his mouth dropped down onto her own gasping one, his hands rushing up to hold her face captive whilst he plunged his tongue in deep.

She kissed him back and kept on coming, her fingers digging into the nape of his neck, her back arching from the bed in some crazed attempt to get closer to him. She felt his release too, deep inside her body; felt the violent shudders of his flesh, felt a flood of heat.

His mouth burst free of hers on a strangled cry of what might have been pain, or pleasure. Their eyes met, Hugh's looking stunned for a moment. But then he laughed.

'Oh, babe,' he said, shaking his head at her. 'You're in big trouble now.'

CHAPTER TWELVE

'YES, I know,' Hugh was saying into his cellphone. 'It's a shame. I was looking forward to tonight as well…Yes, I'm going to go back to bed. And I'm going to stay there all day,' he added with a wink Kathryn's way.

Truly, he was wicked. And a very convincing liar.

'Bye, Fliss. Give my regards to hubbie.'

Hugh shut his phone and put it down on the breakfast bar.

'There,' he said. 'All done. No sailing this afternoon and no dinner party tonight. Now…' He slid off the stool and started making his way round to where she was pouring herself a second cup of coffee.

'You stop right there!' she snapped before he could reach her, or touch her again.

'What?' he said, doing his best to look innocent, not an easy task when he was stark naked. She, at least, was wearing one of his shirts.

'You haven't left me alone since we arrived yesterday afternoon, except for a couple of miserable hours in the middle of the night when I passed out from exhaustion. I need a rest,' she said, resolving to take some control of her life once more. 'I haven't even had anything to eat!'

'Oh, Kathryn, Kathryn,' he said softly. 'Don't go getting all stroppy with me. OK, we'll have a rest for a couple of hours. Though we'll still have to stay here. I can't go out after claiming to all and sundry that I've been struck down by a virus.'

'All and sundry! You only said that to two people. Sydney has a population of over four million!'

'Yes, but Fliss knows everybody who knows everybody and she's an incorrigible gossip. What say I ring up and order us a DVD? I know a place that home delivers. Is there anything particular you'd like to see?'

Kathryn sighed. There went her plans to go home today. Not that she really wanted to, a realisation which flabbergasted her. She'd never been this easy before. Or this…submissive. She had to show Hugh that she wasn't like all those other silly females who fell at his feet. Though she had, hadn't she, in the shower last night?

Oh, God.

'Nothing X-rated,' she said sharply.

'Of course not.'

'And I don't want to watch it in the bedroom.'

'Absolutely not.'

'And you're to go put some clothes on.'

He sighed, turned and trudged off towards the bedroom, making a mockery of his seeming compliance when he returned in a pair of black satin boxer shorts.

'You call that dressed?' she said drily.

'Don't push it, sweetheart.'

Now it was her turn to sigh.

He walked over to pick up his phone once more. 'Have you thought of a movie yet?' he asked as he went through the menu, obviously looking for the video shop's number.

'No. You choose.'

'Fine.'

He surprised her by ordering *Gone with the Wind*, paying for it with his credit card and asking them to deliver it to his post box.

'That's a very long film,' she told him when he hung up.

'Is it? Damn.'

'I'm going to have a shower. Alone this time,' she added quickly before he could suggest otherwise.

His sardonic smile implied it was just a matter of time before she stopped this nonsense.

'I'll rustle us up some breakfast whilst you're gone,' he said.

'Don't tell me you can cook.'

'Not the last time I tried. But I'm a dab hand at pouring muesli and milk. And I can open a bottle of juice like an expert. As for coffee, no one makes better coffee than me,' he finished up, and nodded towards the jar of instant coffee sitting next to the kettle.

'You constantly surprise me,' she said tartly.

'Don't be too long,' he called after her as she left the room.

Hugh muttered under his breath, but he had her measure. She was just running scared, after losing control of her libido last night. Losing control of herself.

He could have done anything with her, could have demanded more.

With other women, he might have. But he'd never felt absolutely certain that they loved doing it. There'd always been that doubt at the back of his mind that if he'd been some ordinary Joe, if he hadn't had billions in the bank, they might not have found him quite so...attractive.

Not once last night had he felt that about Kathryn.

It had been a long time since any female had captivated him to this degree. Hugh had imagined—falsely, as it had turned out—that a sexual marathon with his PA would begin to burn out this mad desire which had been tormenting him these past few weeks. But this morning had found his desire as fierce as ever…

Kathryn was in a quandary over what to put on after her shower. It seemed silly to return to Hugh dressed as if she were going to the office. They were, after all, going to stay here and watch a movie.

In the end, she put the shirt back on she'd been wearing earlier, but with panties underneath this time. She'd brought clean undies with her yesterday when Hugh told her to pack something for an overnight stay. Not much else, though, just her toilet bag.

She didn't bother blow-drying her hair, just pulled it up into a damp pony-tail. Full make-up seemed ridiculous as well, but she did put on some pale pink lipstick.

'You smell nice,' he said on her return to the kitchen.

'It's just my shampoo. It's strawberry-flavoured,' she said stiffly. 'I see you've been busy,' she went on, casting her eyes over the breakfast bar, where he'd set out cereal, fruit and milk, along with appropriate crockery and cutlery.

'Coffee?' he asked, walking over to the kettle.

'Please.' She slid up onto one of the breakfast stools.

He poured them both coffee, then ate standing up and chatting away between mouthfuls in his easy-going and undeniably charming fashion.

'That'll be the DVD arriving,' he said when his cellphone beeped. 'I'll go down and get it.'

'You can't go downstairs dressed in that!' she protested.

He glanced down at his boxer shorts. 'I suppose you're right. How about you?'

'No way!'

He sighed. 'I guess I'll have to put some jeans on.'

He did, but nothing else, going bare-chested downstairs. Oddly enough, she found that look even sexier on him, the tight-fitting jeans sitting low on his hips.

'You're not wearing anything under those, are you?' she said almost accusingly when he returned.

'Nope,' he agreed breezily. 'It's called going commando. Not sure what it's called when ladies do it.'

'Disgusting?' she suggested drily.

He laughed. 'You really are a little hypocrite. You weren't wearing any panties earlier.'

'I am now.'

'More's the pity.'

'Hugh, you promised.'

'What did I promise?'

'To give it a rest for a while.'

'Did I? I don't recall promising anything.'

She gritted her teeth hard in her jaw. 'Don't make me go home.'

His blue eyes narrowed on her. 'No one's making you do anything, Kathryn. I didn't *make* you do anything last night. You wanted me as much as I wanted you. Why don't you admit it?'

'Well, I…'

'There's a chemistry between us,' he swept on before she could formulate a decent defence. 'Why fight it? I tried and it almost damned near drove me insane. I'd have tried to seduce you in the end, even if you'd stayed with Daryl. Even if you'd married him, probably. And I'd have succeeded.'

She just stared at him.

'Don't look at me like that,' he growled. 'Like I told you once before, I'm not a saint. And neither are you. Let's at least be honest with each other. I'll sit and watch that infernal movie with you if that's what you really want. But I'd much rather be making love to you.'

It was extremely seductive, this mad passion he had for her, but also worrying.

'And if I let you do that?' she said. 'What then?'

'What do you mean, what then?'

'You want me to be honest with you. All right. One part of me wants you to make love to me too. The foolish female part. My sensible side is worried sick that if I give you all the sex you want this weekend, then you'll change your mind about marrying me. After all, you only proposed to get into my pants.'

'Now *you're* being crude.'

'No, I'm being honest. I'm nearly thirty years old, Hugh. I've met a lot of men in my time, some of them practised womanisers who will say just about anything to get you into the sack. But once you've come across, they soon go cold on you. The challenge has been met, the mountain climbed and the woman screwed.'

Hugh looked far from pleased at being described as a practised womaniser. But that was what he was, after all.

'There's some element of truth in what you say,' he admitted at last. 'You have been a challenge, Kathryn. And yes, I am hoping that, eventually, I will get over this mad sexual obsession I seemed to have developed where you are concerned. It has, quite frankly, been a pain in the butt.' One corner of his mouth tipped up into a wry smile. 'Unfortunately, it seems where you are concerned that my obsession has now changed into an addiction, for which you only have yourself to blame. You are one hell of a lover, lover. In all honesty, I can't see myself getting bored with you in bed for some considerable time.'

Kathryn tried to keep her head in the face of his perversely flattering words. But it was hard to hold on to common sense when your feminine ego was being stroked with such wicked expertise.

'Still, I can understand your fears,' he went on. 'If you knew me better, you would trust me more. What can I do, I wonder, to reassure you that I will keep my word and marry you?

'I know,' he said before she could think of a thing. 'No more sex today.'

She blinked at him. 'None at all?'

'Absolutely none at all. Come…' He took her hand and led her over to a sofa. 'We will watch *Gone with the Wind* together—not sitting too closely—after which we will talk.'

'Talk,' she repeated blankly.

'Yep. We'll tell each other things. Sit.'

She sat. 'What things?'

'All our deep, dark secrets. We need to become friends, Kathryn.'

'Friends!'

He smiled one of his engaging smiles. 'Is that such an impossibility? That we could become friends? You did say you liked me a little.'

And she wanted to keep it that way. Kathryn suspected that if he kept up this bombardment of charm she would end up liking him a lot more than a little.

'I don't believe you can do it,' she said.

'What—make you my friend, or go the rest of the day without sex?'

'Both,' she said, her chin tilting upwards.

'You really shouldn't challenge me, you know. Russ and Jimmy boy never do any more.'

'You don't want to shag Russ and Jimmy boy,' she pointed out.

He laughed. 'They'll be glad to hear that. Now hush up. We're going to the movies.'

Hugh studied the cover of the DVD for a few seconds before slipping it out of its packet and slotting it into the player.

'You're right,' he said as he returned to sit at the opposite end of the sofa, with the remote in his hand. 'It's a very long movie. Around four hours.'

'I did warn you.'

'I suppose it'll be worth it to find out why that house means so much to you.'

'Scarlett's situation is not the same as mine,' she told him. 'And she's nothing like me.'

The movie started and Scarlett came on the screen, looking glorious in a low-cut dress.

'You're right,' Hugh said after a few minutes. 'She's not like you at all. She's shallow and self-centred and totally empty-headed.'

'But she is beautiful,' Kathryn said, trying not to let his underlying compliments affect her too much.

'Beautiful is as beautiful does. And I don't think she's all that beautiful. Frankly, you leave her for dead.' His head turned, his blue eyes glittering as they moved admiringly over her. 'If Scarlett O'Hara walked into this room right now, I know who I'd prefer.'

What a fool I am, Kathryn thought as she felt herself go to mush.

'Stop talking and watch the movie,' she ordered brusquely.

'Yes, ma'am,' he said, smiling.

Hugh was pleasantly surprised when the story quickly captured his interest. Who would have thought that a movie made all those years ago would stand up so well? Of course, the historical setting helped; stories set back in the old days didn't date as much.

But the setting was just a backdrop, really, the movie's strength coming from the characters and their various relationships. Some of the acting was a little hammy, but not from the two main characters. Scarlett and Rhett were extremely convincing, and their tempestuous relationship very involving. Hugh warmed to Scarlett after a while, despite her being consistently selfish and insensitive. He admired the love she had for her family, and for Tara. Admired the way she mucked in and did whatever needed to be done to survive.

Kathryn had that same courage and strength of character.

When the movie finished, Hugh had no doubt that Scarlett would have got Rhett back. And said as much after he pressed stop on the DVD player.

'Maybe,' Kathryn said.

'*Definitely*. Now, I want to hear all about your own personal Tara. And don't go fobbing me off with that 'it's a long story' excuse. But first, I think we could do with a drink and a snack. That really was a long movie. But I don't want to spoil our appetite for dinner. I'm planning on getting in some Chinese. The local restaurant home-delivers, too. You like Chinese, I hope.'

'Yes.'

'Great. Meanwhile, how do champagne and nibbles sound to you? We could take them out on the balcony, soak up some sun and while away the rest of the afternoon getting pleasantly sozzled and telling each other our life stories.'

Kathryn wasn't sure she'd be going that far. She was not an habitual confider, like some girls. She'd learned to keep secrets during her childhood. Learned not to make friends as well, habits which had continued into adulthood.

When past boyfriends had asked why she didn't take them home, she'd lied, saying that her parents were dead. This was only half true. Her father was long dead, but till a couple of years back her mother was alive. In a fashion.

Daryl was the only boyfriend she'd told about her upbringing. Firstly, because by then her mother had passed away—from renal failure—and also because he'd had a similar problem when he'd been growing up.

Looking back, however, Daryl had not been all that sympathetic, telling her that lots of kids were worse off than her and it was high time she got over it. After all, she hadn't been beaten up, had she? Or sexually abused. He couldn't understand the pain—and the shame—she'd suffered at the hands of her mentally-ill mother.

Kathryn couldn't see Hugh understanding, either. Not many people understood bipolar disorder.

But he seemed determined to find out why Val's house meant so much to her and, given the circumstances, Kathryn supposed he had a right to know.

'OK,' he said once they were installed on his balcony, champagne in hand and a big dish of honey and soy crisps on the table between them. 'Shoot.'

Kathryn took a sip of bubbly whilst wondering where exactly to start. With her parents' extremely heavy drug addiction perhaps, which had led to her father being jailed for dealing and her brain-damaged mother left behind to raise her, their two-year-old daughter? Or should she jump to the years after her father had been beaten to death in prison, when her by then drug-free but bipolar mother was still totally unable to cope with day-to-day living, let alone the needs of a school-age child?

Kathryn could still remember the first day she'd gone to school. Not on the first day that all the other children had started, of course. Her mother hadn't remembered to take her then.

Kathryn had been two days late. Her uniform had been second-hand and way too big for her emaciated frame. Her lunch had been two Vegemite sandwiches, carried in a plastic bag.

The really tragic thing was that she hadn't been upset by any of this. She was used to her mother's neglect and hadn't known any different. But the children in her class had soon made her realise she was very different indeed.

She had quickly become the object of their scorn. She'd been teased and tormented. Not bashed, but emotionally bullied.

The teacher hadn't seemed to have any pity on her. Neither had she said anything to anyone about the days Kathryn didn't go to school—the days when her mother hadn't been able to get out of bed.

School had become a misery. It was no wonder her grades had been hopeless back then. How could she have learnt anything when she'd spent every day there in a state of stomach-churning anxiety?

'By the look on your face,' Hugh said, 'things must have been very bad for you as a kid.'

She turned to look at him. To really look at him. Not as her devilishly handsome, wickedly sexy boss, but as a person, a fellow human being whose eyes weren't just beautiful, but also very kind.

'Yes,' she choked out, 'they were.'

'You don't have to tell me if you don't want to,' he said gently. 'But if you do, I promise I won't judge, or make facile comments. I'll just listen.'

Which he did, amazingly, not saying a word as she did her best to paint a picture of her life before Val.

'I desperately wanted a friend,' she explained at one stage. 'But I couldn't have one, even if by some miracle anyone had wanted to befriend me. I could never take anyone home, you see. You've no idea what it was like there, Hugh. The place was always a shambles. Because of her illness, my mother had become a hoarder. There was wall-to-wall junk in every room. I was ashamed of it...and ashamed of her.'

When tears pricked at her eyes, Kathryn quickly brushed them aside. 'Sorry. No point in crying. Look, to cut this long story short again, one day—it was during Easter, just after I'd turned nine—a man from the Salvation Army knocked on our door. In hindsight, someone must have called them and said we needed help. I don't know who. A neighbour perhaps. Anyway, I'll never forget the shocked look on his face when he walked inside. I'd never felt so ashamed. But, really, he was very sweet and kind. When my mum started crying he put his arm around her and said that he'd help her fix the place up. But he added that it really wasn't a fit place for a little girl. And then he did the most wonderful thing of all. He sent me to Val's place for the rest of the holidays.'

Kathryn smiled at that memory. 'Val had been having needy and neglected kids for holidays ever since she'd become a widow, I eventually found out. That holiday, however, there was just me and her.'

'How old was she back then?' Hugh asked.

'When I first met Val she was sixty-five. But she seemed younger. She was so full of life. Yet she'd had a sad life, really. Her only two children—both boys—had died in accidents. One when he was twelve. He fell out of a tree, a Norfolk pine. The second one was killed in a motorcycle crash when he was eighteen. She told me they'd been just like their father: thrill-seekers. Her husband had also died in an accident, you see. He'd bought a gyrocopter for his fiftieth birthday and crashed it on his first flight. Silly bugger he was, Val used to say.'

'People say I'm just like my father, too,' Hugh remarked drily.

Kathryn frowned. 'In what way? You don't look like him.'

'No, I take after Mum with my looks. Though I get my height from Dad. And, according to him, my intelligence. I suspect, however, when people say I'm a chip off the old block, they're referring to my inability to commit to one woman, a flaw which I recognised shortly after I hit puberty. By the time I reached eighteen I'd had about fifty girlfriends. I decided then and there never to follow dear old Dad's example and buy a wedding ring every time I fell into lust.'

'Till now,' Kathryn said before she could think better of it.

Hugh just laughed. '*Touché*. So you'd better make it worth my while, lover. But back to your story. Tell me more about your relationship with Val and about her house.'

'Gosh, it's really hard to explain to someone like you.'

'I don't see why.'

'You wouldn't appreciate what it meant to me to live in a clean house with someone who was prepared to play games with you and to listen to you. Every evening we used to sit out on the verandah and eat ice cream together, after which we'd play I-spy. I'd never had that kind of attention before.'

'You probably won't believe me,' Hugh said, 'but I suffered from a lack of that kind of personal attention too. My father was always too busy to play with me. He never came to sports day or awards day at school. He certainly never listened to anything I had to say.'

'But you still had your mother,' Kathryn pointed out. 'I would imagine she was a very good mother.'

'Then you'd imagine wrong. After the divorce, my mother suffered depression for years. She often didn't get out of bed all day, just like your mother. And she drank too much. But you're right, I didn't have to tolerate a dirty house, or wearing unwashed clothes. There was always paid staff to tend to such matters. The housekeeper used to check that I'd cleaned behind my ears and brushed my teeth every night.'

'Would you believe that before I went to Val's I'd never cleaned my teeth?'

'My God, Kathryn, that's deplorable!'

'Val was horrified too. She whipped me off to the dentist and had them properly checked out and cleaned. The dentist said I was very lucky that I had naturally good teeth and hadn't eaten too many lollies. After that, Val took me to the dentist every Christmas holidays and paid for it herself.'

'What a wonderful woman,' Hugh said.

'She was. Yet she wasn't a pushover. She didn't do everything for me. She made me do things for myself. Val had a list of rules up on the kitchen wall which every kid who went there had to adhere to. We had to make our own beds, clean our rooms, help clean the rest of the house, do the washing-up. Things like that. But I didn't mind. I loved it all. She gave me the tools to survive when I went home. She taught me how to clean and how to cook, and how to look after myself. I couldn't do much about the mess Mum kept making when I was out of the house, but I kept my own room spotlessly clean. Each time Val used to send me home with a big supply of cleaning products and toiletries which I stashed under my bed and eked out till I went back to her place the next time. Trust me when I say that I have never, ever missed one night brushing my teeth since.'

Hugh smiled over at her. 'I believe you.'

She sighed. 'I know I'm a pain in the neck when it comes to being organised and disciplined. But maybe now you understand why. I have to have order in my life, Hugh. I have to have goals and plans.'

'And you have to have Val's house,' he finished up for her.

'I guess I would have survived without it.'

'But not as happily.'

'No.'

They both fell silent for a minute or two.

'I have a confession to make,' Hugh finally piped up.

Kathryn glanced over at him. 'What?'

'Remember earlier when you said you didn't think I could make you my friend and not have sex with you today?'

'Yes,' she said warily.

'You were right. I *am* going to go to bed with you. Right now,' he added, and put his champagne glass down.

'Oh…' She swallowed, her stomach instantly tight.

He stood up and walked around to her chair. 'If I learned one thing from watching *Gone with the Wind*,' he growled, twisting the chair away from the table then scooping her up into his arms, 'it's never to ask for sex. Much better to just take. And take. And take…'

CHAPTER THIRTEEN

'I REALLY should be going home soon,' Kathryn said.

Hugh leant further back into his corner of the triangular-shaped spa bath, his arms stretching out along the blue-tiled surrounds.

'Why?' he asked.

'It's getting late.'

'Not that late.' Hugh wasn't exactly sure of the time but the sun had only just gone down. They'd spent most of Saturday night and a good percentage of Sunday having the most incredible sex, till an exhausted Kathryn had finally fallen asleep on top of his bed a couple of hours back.

Hugh had spent the time she'd been unconscious watching her and wanting her still. It was weird, he'd thought, that he couldn't seem to get enough of her. Normally, once he'd had a woman as much as he'd already had Kathryn, he would begin to grow bored with her.

But not this time.

He only had to touch her and his desire would begin to return. Kissing her was an instant remedy for any temporary tiredness. Her kissing him fired him up with enough power to rocket to the moon.

After an hour and a half's increasingly impatient waiting, Hugh had run a deep bubble bath, ignoring Kathryn's protests when he'd scooped her sleepy, naked body up off the bed and carried her into the bathroom.

She hadn't protested for long.

Now, as he sat in the bath, watching her with hungry eyes, Hugh wondered if this was the type of lust which had consistently tricked his father into thinking he was in love. Hugh had to admit that it was pretty powerful stuff.

But being forewarned was forearmed. As much as he admired and desired Kathryn, Hugh knew that his mad passion for her would eventually wane. It was just a matter of time.

That time, however, had not come yet.

'Why don't you stay another night?' he suggested.

Kathryn groaned as she struggled with instant temptation. She wanted to stay. Of course she did. Hugh was a brilliant lover. Imaginative, skilful and amazingly virile.

The trouble lay with her.

'I can't, Hugh,' she said, doing her best to sound firm.

'Why not?'

Kathryn shook her head. 'I just can't.'

His face showed frustration. 'I thought we'd got past that kind of answer, Kathryn. We promised each other total honesty this weekend, remember?'

'You won't like my answer.'

'How do you know?'

She laughed. 'I know.'

'Try me.'

Kathryn realised then that brutal honesty might just work for her. Once Hugh heard what she had to say, he might cool things a bit.

'All right,' she said. 'The thing is, Hugh, I've realised over the last few days that I have this problem when it comes to sex.'

'Really? I didn't notice that you had any problems at all. You're the most uninhibited girl that I've ever been with.'

Kathryn sighed an exasperated sigh. 'I'm not talking about the physical side of sex. I'm talking about the way sex makes me *feel*.'

'Which is?'

'It seems that when I'm sexually attracted to a man, soon or later I begin to think I'm in love with them. Especially after I've been to bed with them. The better the sex, the stronger my emotional involvement. Daryl was good in bed, you see. That's why I thought I loved him. But you, Hugh, you're the best lover I've ever had, by far.'

She watched his expression change from a smug satisfaction to a dawning apprehension. 'Hell, Kathryn, are you saying you think you're in love with me?'

'No,' she said. 'Not yet. But I'm only human, Hugh. And rather vulnerable right now. I really don't want to start thinking I'm in love with you.'

'I don't want you to start thinking you're in love with me, either,' he said, sounding horrified at the thought.

'I do realise that,' came her tart reply. 'That's why I think we should cool things a bit.'

He looked at her for a long time with eyes that were far from cool.

'Would it help if I became a more selfish lover?' he suggested. 'No foreplay, no pillow talk, no pillows at all, actually. I'll take you up against walls and on desks and in lifts. Make sure you don't enjoy it too much.'

Heat flamed in her cheeks as he mentioned the very places and ways in which she'd already fantasised his having his way with her. She glanced away for fear of his seeing the excitement in her eyes.

'I take it that suggestion won't exactly cool things down for you?' he said, his voice tinged with humour.

When her eyes turned back to his, she saw the knowing glitter in them.

'Would there be any point in my denying it?' She shook her head from side to side as the reality of the situation swamped her. 'You've totally corrupted me, Hugh.'

'I haven't corrupted you, sweetheart. You're a perfectly normal woman with a strong libido. That's nothing to be ashamed of. Far too many girls think they should be in love to enjoy being made love to. That's total rubbish. So just relax now and enjoy what I have to offer you,' he said as he pried her legs apart with his foot. 'It feels good, doesn't it?'

Kathryn stiffened when she felt his foot sliding up her inner leg, her hands gripping the sides of the bath once his toes made intimate contact at the apex of her thighs.

'You like?' he asked in husky tones after a minute of the most exquisite toe torture.

Kathryn swallowed, then nodded.

'You'll like this better,' he said.

With a few deft movements he slipped both his legs under hers, lifting her knees as he scooped forward in the water and entered her. *He was so right*, she thought as her arms automatically reached to wrap around his neck, her legs finding a home around his waist, both actions pulling him deeper into her already turned-on body. *She liked this much better.*

'Damn,' he muttered.

She blinked. 'What is it?'

'I forgot the condom.'

'Does it matter? I promise you I won't get pregnant.'

'That's not the point,' Hugh retorted. 'I always use a condom.'

'In that case, everything's perfectly safe. And it does feel good, doesn't it?' she said, wiggling her bottom.

Too good, Hugh thought as he took firm hold of her hips. His first intention was to keep her still, then to withdraw. But his hands had other ideas and before he knew it he was rocking her back and forth.

'Oh, yes,' she said, then moved herself without any help.

Hugh groaned as the tension began to build. And build. Her flesh started squeezing him tightly, her eyelids growing heavy as her head tipped back and her lips fell wantonly apart.

He wasn't the one who'd corrupted her, Hugh decided as he watched her come with wild abandon. She'd corrupted him.

His own climax was just as violent, Hugh wallowing in the alien experience of pumping hot and free into her lush, greedy flesh. With any other woman, he might have worried that she was trying to trap him with a pregnancy. His father had drummed that warning into him from his teenage years.

And he'd heeded that warning. Till tonight.

But Hugh knew Kathryn wasn't that kind of girl.

She didn't want him, or his baby, or his money for that matter. She wanted a decent man to love her and marry her, and to stay married to her for the rest of her life. She wanted commitment and caring and security for herself, and her children.

All she wants from you, Hugh, my boy—other than that vital piece of paper—is sex.

Which is exactly all you want from her, he reminded himself sternly when an oddly emotional lump filled his throat.

So stop being stupid and get on with it.

'I think it's time we went back to bed,' he said, and pulled the bath plug out from under her.

CHAPTER FOURTEEN

'HUGH PARKINSON'S office. Kathryn Hart speaking. How may I help you?'

'Kathryn, dear. Good morning. By any chance is Hugh there?'

It was Hugh's mother. Normally, Kathryn would have been totally at ease with the woman. Today, however, she could not bring herself to be her usual sweet self.

'Sorry, Mrs Parkinson. He's playing golf.'

'I thought as much. I know he plays every Thursday morning. I did try his mobile but it's turned off. Which is rather silly, given his position at the moment. What if something important came up and you wanted to contact him?'

'I have mentioned that to him, Mrs Parkinson,' Kathryn said with an edge in her voice.

'Yes, dear, I'm sure you have,' she said cheerfully. 'He must be a very frustrating man to work for.'

Very, Kathryn thought, Hugh having not made love to her once this week. He'd stunned her on Monday morning by saying that he would now wait till the following Sunday; that, thanks to her being so accommodating over the weekend, he was no longer off the planet with uncontrollable lust. He'd given her a patronising kiss on the cheek and told her that she didn't have to worry about his not going through with the marriage, because he wasn't cured yet, just temporarily appeased.

If anything had been designed to give Kathryn a reality check it was that kiss, so unlike the kisses they'd shared the previous day, the long, hungry, intimate kisses which he'd bestowed all over her body—and vice versa.

One part of her—the common-sense part—had reasoned it was all for the best. Because by the time he'd finally taken her home on Sunday evening, she'd begun having strongly sentimental feelings towards him.

The last thing Kathryn wanted was to start thinking she'd fallen for him. So she should have been relieved that Hugh had decided to cool things for a while.

Her revved-up libido, however, hadn't been happy at all.

But she'd just said 'fine', as if she didn't really care whether they slept together or not.

Which was not true at all, their passionate weekend together having evoked a lust in her which was cruel in its intensity. She could not look at him without being consumed with sexual craving.

Which was why she was not in the best of moods that Thursday morning. Three days and nights of intense frustration had left her feeling somewhat…frazzled.

'Could I leave a message with you for Hugh?' his mother asked.

'Of course,' came her brusque reply.

'Tell him that lunch tomorrow is back on. I'll drop by the office at twelve-thirty. I've made a booking for one at a new place. It's just a short walk from the Parkinson building.'

'I'll tell him, Mrs Parkinson. Is there anything else?'

'No…no…nothing. Er—see you tomorrow, dear.'

Kathryn hung up, then sighed. She hoped she hadn't sounded rude.

But it was difficult to be bright and happy when you weren't either. Her eyes went to her wristwatch. It was half-past eleven. Hugh would be finishing his golf game soon.

She wondered what his friends would say when he asked them to be witnesses at their wedding. She hoped they gave him a hard time. He deserved it.

'Now that we're alone for a minute,' James said. 'what do you really think about Hugh marrying his PA because of some ridiculous will?'

Russell had been thinking of nothing else since Hugh had told them of his amazing marital plans as the three of them walked up the fairway to the eighteenth green.

'I'm not sure,' Russell said slowly, glancing over his shoulder to check that Hugh was still at the bar inside, buying the post-golf drinks. The fact that Hugh had once again played atrocious golf showed that their friend was not himself. Hadn't been for quite some time.

'It's not unlike Hugh to be kind,' Russell went on. 'You know what a soft touch he is. He's donated heaps of money to Nicole's orphanage in Bangkok. But acts of monetary generosity are a far cry from entering into a secret marriage. I have to confess that I think there's more to this than meets the eye.'

'My feelings exactly,' James said. 'What do you know about this PA of his? I've never met her. Have you?'

'Strangely enough, no. I only know what Hugh has told us about her. I always got the impression he found her a right pain in the neck. Now I'm beginning to wonder if she's been engendering pain in a much lower area of his body.'

'Hugh would never marry a woman just for sex,' James said.

'Why not? His father does it all the time.'

'True. But Hugh said this was a marriage in name only. And it's not like Hugh to lie.'

'Everyone lies, especially when it comes to relationships. I lied to Nicole when I first met her. And you, my friend, have done nothing but lie to your Megan.'

James shrugged. 'I haven't hurt her. She's very happy.'

Russell could not deny that Megan did seem happy. The two married couples often went out together, so he'd had plenty of opportunity to observe Megan. Of course, the poor girl believed her husband loved her. But he didn't. James was still hung up on his ex-wife.

More fool him, Russell thought. Megan was worth ten of Jackie. But James couldn't seem to see that.

His marrying Megan just to have the family Jackie couldn't give him had been an extremely ruthless thing to do, especially the way he'd seduced and impregnated the poor girl *before* he proposed. Hugh had been even more appalled than Russell over their friend's actions, and had been very vocal on the subject. Despite his having garnered a well-deserved reputation as a serial womaniser, Hugh was a closet romantic. He believed marriage should not be entered into for any other reason than true love, the kind which lasted forever. Since he believed himself incapable of such love, he'd made the decision many years ago never to marry.

Yet next Sunday afternoon he was going to do just that.

It didn't really add up.

'I think Hugh is lying to us,' Russell said.

'Maybe. Maybe not. We'll have a better idea on Sunday, when we meet the woman in question. In the meantime, we'll make sure that he's taken every precaution to protect himself against a potential gold-digger.'

'My God, you think she might be after his money?'

'Could be. That house and will story could be a complete fabrication. I wonder if Hugh has actually seen this will for himself.'

'He's not a complete fool, James.'

'Or even a partial one,' the man himself said drily as he put the three glasses of beer on the table then sat down in his chair. 'Kathryn signed a foolproof pre-nup yesterday.'

Russell tried to read something in Hugh's face, but failed. One of Hugh's many talents was as a poker player. The only clue Russell had was Hugh's sudden loss of form on the golf course. It was extremely difficult to play good golf when one was emotionally or physically distracted.

Russell suddenly remembered Hugh telling him at James's wedding last year that there was a woman he fancied who wouldn't come across.

Could that woman be his PA?

It wouldn't be the first time that a boss had become enamoured of his secretary. The two were thrown together a lot, after all.

'Is Kathryn beautiful?' he suddenly asked his friend.

Hugh took a long swallow of beer before answering. He knew his friends would give him the third degree over this. Knew they would be shocked, and then worried if he admitted to a sexual relationship with Kathryn.

That's why he'd delayed telling them till today. And why he'd decided to lie to them.

'Not in a strictly traditional sense,' he replied.

'Attractive, though.'

'Yes. Quite attractive.'

'Blonde?'

'No. Brunette.'

Russell frowned. Hugh was being cagey all right. Which wasn't like him. He decided to play the devil's advocate. 'You do realise your marriage won't be legal if you don't consummate it.'

There was a definite flicker in Hugh's eyes.

'How will anyone know if we did or not? Kathryn's no virgin. I don't know what you're so worried about. I'm just helping her out.'

'I thought you didn't like her,' James piped up.

'She can be irritating,' Hugh admitted. 'She has a tendency to be bossy and controlling. But she's a good person. And she's been badly done by with this stupid will. *And* an even stupider fiancé. Well, ex-fiancé now. Look, the one thing I haven't mentioned so far is that I feel personally responsible for the break-up of her engagement.'

'How come?' Russell asked, suspicion in his voice.

'Remember I had a board meeting last Thursday afternoon? Anyway, Kathryn's fiancé was supposed to take her out to dinner that night but, at the last moment, he let her down. So I took her to dinner. By way of a thank-you for all her hard work.'

James and Russell exchanged knowing looks.

'It wasn't like that,' Hugh snapped. 'It was a perfectly innocent dinner. But her fiancé was the jealous type. Unfortunately, I drove Kathryn home. After he saw her get out of my car he apparently went crazy, called her vile names and hit her.'

'Charming,' James said with a curl of his top lip. He despised men who hit women.

'She's better off without him,' Hugh said. 'Not, however, better off without her friend's house. It's difficult to explain why without revealing rather sensitive and very confidential information. Let me just say that she—'

'Where did you take her to dinner?' Russell broke in abruptly.

'What? What has that got to do with anything?'

'Just curious.'

'Neptune's.'

'Aah…' Russell knew Hugh's *modus operandi* with women he fancied. The first place he ever took them was Neptune's.

Hugh saw the speculation in Russell's eyes. But speculation was not knowledge.

'I gather you two think this marriage is a foolish step on my part,' he said. 'Please be assured that I know what I'm doing. When you meet Kathryn for yourself, you'll soon see that I haven't become the target of some conniving fortune-hunter.'

'I hope you've got your stories off pat when the Press find out,' James warned.

'They shouldn't find out, not unless one of you blab.'

'*We* won't. We won't even tell our wives. But what about Reverend What's-his-name?'

'I donate thousands to the Reverend Price's halfway house every year. Trust me. He won't breathe a word.'

'Someone always finds out, Hugh.'

Not if I can help it, Hugh determined on his drive back to the office. When this was all over—and it would be once Kathryn inherited Val's house—he didn't want to have to answer some journalist's stupid questions. He wanted to forget that Kathryn Hart had ever existed, and just get back to his life as it had once been.

She'd caused him more trouble than any woman ever had. Hell, he'd even started thinking that he might have actually fallen in love with her.

This patently ridiculous idea had come over him when

he'd been making love to her. No, she'd been making love to him, very late last Sunday. He'd reached down to run his fingers through her hair. Her head had lifted, their eyes had met and pow! He'd been zapped by an emotion previously unknown to him. A violently possessive, powerfully protective, infinitely loving feeling which had shocked him so much that he'd pushed her head back down almost roughly, not stopping her as he usually did.

It had proved a relief, afterwards, that she'd refused to stay another night, Hugh taking her home shortly after that episode. He'd needed time to think.

By morning Hugh had made the difficult decision to call a halt to their affair. He still wanted her like crazy, but at the time he had wanted more to find out if his experience the previous evening was the same kind of delusion which regularly took possession of his father. He reasoned that if he ever looked at Kathryn and was consumed by the same emotions when *not* engaged in sexual activity, then that would be conclusive.

The next day at work, Hugh had been perversely dismayed when he'd walked into the office and felt not some overwhelming wave of love, but that same old irritating surge of desire. He'd been even more irritated by Kathryn's reaction when he told her there would be no more sex till they were married.

If he'd been secretly thinking—or foolishly hoping—that she might be falling for him, then he'd been dead wrong.

But brother, her offhand attitude had tempted him severely to retract what he'd said and demand she follow him into the inner sanctum immediately, where he would shag her silly on his father's desk.

Only his pride had stopped him.

Things had gone from bad to worse after that, his desire for her mounting each day, his mind a mess, his sleep constantly interrupted by wildly erotic dreams.

No wonder his golf game had been pathetic this morning.

Kathryn must have slept well, however, Hugh noted ruefully when he strode into the office just after midday. She looked fine, and sexy as all hell in that black suit which had always tormented him, the one he'd fantasised stripping off her so many times. She was wearing a silky red cami under it today, and her lips were glossed the same colour.

Why he was keeping to his stupid no-sex rule he had no idea. What was the point? It was perfectly obvious that he hadn't fallen for her. And she certainly had fallen for him.

When her eyes lifted to meet his, they were nothing like the way her eyes had been with him last weekend. They didn't caress him, or cling to his. The only emotion they betrayed was curiosity.

'What did your friends say?' she asked straight away. 'Were they shocked?'

'Suspicious more than shocked,' he retorted. 'Of you.'

'Me!'

'They obviously think you're a gold-digger,' he said, and strode on into his father's office.

Kathryn followed him. 'Didn't you explain about Val's will and everything?'

'Of course. They didn't buy it.'

'Oh, dear.'

'It doesn't matter what they think, Kathryn,' he said impatiently. 'What matters is what I think. And I know you're no gold-digger. Now, I'm going upstairs to have a shower and change. I'm all sweaty after golf.'

'Your mother called,' she said before he could escape.

'What about?'

'She complained that your mobile was turned off.'

Hugh sighed, pulled his phone out and turned it back on.

'Anything else?' he asked as he returned the phone to his pocket.

'She said lunch tomorrow was back on. She's booked some place that's within walking distance and she'll be here to pick you up at twelve-thirty.'

'Fine. Any other messages whilst we're at it?'

'No. Nothing important. So...did you win? At golf?'

His laugh was scornful. 'Hardly. I played like a dromedary.'

'Why?'

He stared at her hard. If she didn't know why, then she didn't have one intuitive bone in her body. Couldn't she feel his desire? Wasn't it hitting her in waves?

'I was thinking of you,' he said, having reached that point of no return again. 'Thinking of you, back here, sitting at your desk stark naked, your legs apart, with my mouth between them.'

He watched with dark triumph at the way her eyes widened, then glittered. So she wasn't as cool as she was pretending to be.

He smiled his satisfaction. 'Now that I'm here, however, I have a different fantasy. Come share my shower with me,' he said, and held out his hand towards her.

She didn't move. 'But you said that...'

'I know what I said,' he snapped. 'I've changed my mind.'

Still, she didn't move.

No way was he going to let her reject him. No way!

'Don't make me blackmail you again, Kathryn,' he growled. 'Come with me of your own free will. Do it because you want to, not because you're forced to.'

Something flickered in her eyes. He wasn't sure what.

'I...I have to turn on the answering machine first,' she said with a deliciously telling tremor to her voice. 'And lock the door. We can't just leave the office unattended and wide open.'

'I'll wait.'

Kathryn could not believe how turned-on she was. Even before she came back into his office. Even before he pulled her into his arms and kissed her, long and hard. He didn't make small talk for once, just led her upstairs to his father's penthouse and into the guest-room *en suite*, where he undressed her very slowly and very silently.

She was trembling by the time she stood, naked, before him.

'Now *you* undress *me*,' he said, breaking his silence at last.

He had to help her a little with his top, his being so tall. But he let her do the rest. When she went down on her knees to remove his shoes and socks, he groaned. When she finally pushed his underpants downwards, releasing his erection, he groaned again. But when she went to touch him he said 'No' sharply and spun away to turn on the shower taps.

Hugh chose a green shower gel which smelt faintly of apple, pouring a generous amount into the middle of the sea sponge before handing it to her.

'Wash me well, wench,' he ordered in a gravelly voice. 'Like I said, I'm sweaty from golf.'

It was the most erotic thing she'd ever done, washing him well, her heartbeat galloping as she stroked the soap-slicked sponge over his shoulders and chest before rubbing it over his taut stomach, then sliding it down lower. His sex seemed to swell even further under her hand, its obvious excitement calling to her to kneel down and take it into her mouth.

Her lips tightened around him and he came, crying out with raw pleasure as his seed flowed freely into the heat of her mouth.

She didn't mind. She didn't care. She was off in another world where she would have done anything to please him, anything at all…

CHAPTER FIFTEEN

IT HAD happened again, Hugh thought almost despairingly as he leant back against the tiles. That rush of emotion, that dreadfully weak, intensely loving feeling when he'd wanted to yank her to her feet and crush her to him and tell her, No, I don't want you to do that. I want to make love to you properly. I want to be inside you. I want to see your eyes.

Even as he drew her up onto her feet, he still wanted that.

But it isn't true love, he reminded himself forcefully as he watched her tip her face up into the spray. Because it only happened to him during sex. It was, however, extremely convincing and confusing. He could almost understand his father for marrying because of it.

Hell, *he* was marrying because of it. Kathryn had been right about that. Still, he knew it wouldn't last, this feeling. Or their marriage. It was nothing but a convenience, to both of them.

But a brilliantly satisfying convenience, provided they could both keep their heads and not start imagining things.

Moving her away from the shower spray, he smoothed her wet hair back from her face and looked deep into her still dilated eyes.

'Pity my golf game wasn't tomorrow,' he said. 'I might have played better.'

'I haven't been able to concentrate either,' she admitted in a rather shaken voice.

It worried him slightly, that admission. 'You haven't started thinking you've fallen in love with me, have you?'

Her soft laugh reassured him. 'I've hated you all week.'

'Because you wanted more sex?'

'Yes,' she choked out. 'All the time.'

'Shall we take the rest of the afternoon off?'

'We shouldn't…'

'But we will,' he said, smiling as he turned off the taps.

But he'd only managed to wrap her in a towel when he heard the sound of his mobile ringing.

'Damn,' he muttered, thinking he should not have turned the wretched thing on. He was one of those people who couldn't ignore a phone. He simply had to answer it.

'Sorry,' he said to Kathryn as he scooped his trousers off the floor and fished the phone out of the pocket.

It was Russ.

'What's up, buddy?'

Russ sighed an unhappy-sounding sigh. 'Bad news, I'm afraid. Megan's had a miscarriage. I tried to ring you earlier but your mobile was turned off.'

'Poor Megan,' Hugh said.

'It's James I'm worried about, Hugh. I've never seen him this distraught.'

Hugh didn't say a word. His sympathies all lay with Megan.

'Do you think you could come to the hospital?' Russ went on. 'Offer the poor bloke some words of comfort?'

Hugh pulled a face. 'I don't think that's such a good idea, Russ. You know what I thought of his marrying that girl.'

'That's irrelevant now, Hugh. He's still your friend and he needs you. You're so much better at sympathy than I am.'

Hugh sighed. Russ was right. It wasn't his place to judge. 'OK. What hospital?'

'Belleview Hill Private. Do you know where it is?'

'Nope. But my car's got a satellite navigation system. I'll find it. See you soon, Russ. Bye.'

'I'm truly sorry, Kathryn, but I have to go,' he said, grabbing a towel and drying himself with rapid strokes. 'One of my golfing buddies. His wife's had a miscarriage.'

'You're talking about James Logan, aren't you?'

'Yep.'

'I didn't realise he'd married again.'

'He shouldn't have. He's still in love with his first wife. She divorced him when she couldn't have children.'

'Why didn't they just adopt?'

'Apparently she didn't want to.'

'That seems a bit silly.'

Hugh frowned. Yes, he supposed it was.

'Whatever,' he said, shrugging. 'It was still very wrong to marry a girl he didn't love, just to have children. But I'll try not to point that out to him today. He must be feeling pretty terrible.'

'Yes, he must.'

'Look, from the sounds of things Jim's in a pretty bad way, so I'll probably spend a few hours with him. Why don't you take the rest of the afternoon off? Go shopping. Keep your mobile on and I'll give you a ring when I can. Or, if you like, you could take a taxi to my place. I'll give you my key.'

Kathryn knew she should say no to this last suggestion. She hadn't lied when she'd said she'd been hating him all week. She had. But that hate had evaporated the moment he'd taken her into his arms. Now, as she looked at him, she wasn't craving his body so much. She just wanted more of his company.

The thought of going shopping did not appeal. The thought of going home to an empty flat appealed even less.

'If I go to your place,' Kathryn said carefully as she began dressing, 'I don't want to stay the whole night.'

'That's fine. I'll drive you home at some stage.'

'Do you want me to cook you dinner?'

'No. Just meet me at the door with nothing on but your high heels.'

She blinked, then laughed. 'OK,' she said, thinking it was impossible to fall in love with a man who didn't want anything from you but sex.

Once they were both dressed, Kathryn accompanied him downstairs, where he gave her his key and a goodbye kiss.

'I've decided to hold the fort here for a while,' she said. 'If I don't hear from you by four-thirty, I'll take a taxi to your place.'

When he drew a fifty-dollar note out of his wallet, she shook her head. 'No, thank you, Hugh. I like to pay my own way.'

He smiled a wry smile as he repocketed his money. 'If we were getting married for real, I'd have to re-educate you, Kat, darling. At the moment you're not cut out to be the wife of a billionaire.'

'But you're not a billionaire, Hugh. Your father's the billionaire.'

Hugh almost corrected her, but decided not to. She might panic if she knew just how personally rich he was.

'And I thought we agreed, no more of those Kat darlings,' she went on rather snippily.

Hugh rolled his eyes. 'Thank goodness you're going to divorce me as quickly as possible,' he shot back. 'Because you're one hell of a nag.'

'So I've been told.'

'The only time you're nice is when you're making love.'

'Is that so?' she said, crossing her arms.

'Yeah, that's so.'

'And you're only nice when you *want* to make love,' she pointed out archly.

'Rubbish! I'm nice all the time. Now hush up, Kat, darling,' he said, and swept her into his arms, where he gave her an impassioned and quite mind-numbing kiss.

'Much better,' he said as he let her go. 'I can see that the only way with you is to keep that sarcastic mouth of yours occupied at all times. There are several bottles of very good wine in my fridge,' he called back over his shoulder as he headed for the door. 'Feel free to open one. See you.'

CHAPTER SIXTEEN

'HUGH…'

Hugh glanced up from the menu he was studying. 'Yes, Mum?'

'What's going on between you and Kathryn?'

Hugh adopted a superbly puzzled expression. 'What do you mean?'

'You know exactly what I mean,' she replied shortly. 'Don't try that innocent face on me. Your father used to do exactly that, and when he did I always knew he was lying. You're sleeping with that girl. Don't bother to deny it. I am a very intuitive woman. *And* very observant. Did you think I wouldn't notice your PA wasn't wearing her engagement ring? On top of that, she wasn't herself with me just now. Same thing when I rang yesterday. She was agitated. And, usually, Kathryn is never agitated.'

Hugh decided that an edited version of the truth would suffice. 'She's broken up with her fiancé,' he said. 'The low-life hit her.'

His mother looked shocked. 'Oh, the poor thing. I hope you gave him what for.'

Hugh smiled. 'I did indeed. And then, of course, Kathryn naturally needed some comforting.'

'Hugh, you didn't!'

Hugh began to feel slightly impatient with her. 'Mum, for pity's sake, you know what the men in our family are like where women are concerned. As you so rightly pointed out last week, I've been fancying Kathryn for quite some time.'

'But to seduce her on the rebound!'

'What better time to seduce a woman? If I'd waited, I might not have been successful. After all, Kathryn doesn't really like me all that much. She thinks I'm spoiled, arrogant and totally selfish.'

'Which you obviously are!'

'Yes, well, we can't all be perfect. Don't worry. Our affair won't last for long.'

'That's why it's so deplorable. That poor girl is sure to fall in love with you.'

'I doubt it.'

'Oh truly! You simply don't understand women any better than your father does. I was talking to him earlier today and—'

'You were talking to Dad?' Hugh broke in, startled by this revelation.

'He rings me up every time he splits with his current wife.'

Hugh's stomach contracted. 'Don't tell me he's bored with Krystal already,' he bit out. 'They've only been married a year.'

'You haven't heard from him, I gather.'

'No.' Hugh could feel rage welling up inside him.

'You will. He's planning to fly home tomorrow.'

'I see,' Hugh said with cold anger in his voice. 'And what was the reason he gave for the break-up this time?' His father usually said he'd just fallen out of love, and life was too short to stay married to someone you didn't love.

'I gather it was Krystal who left him, not the other way around.'

'Wanted to cash in early, did she?'

'No, she found out Dickie had had a vasectomy.'

Hugh shook his head from side to side. 'And when did he do that?'

'After you were born. He didn't tell me at the time, of course. He let me think we could have more children. I didn't find out till years later, when he probably thought it wouldn't hurt me.'

'What an unconscionable bastard he is.'

'Quite. And if you don't watch yourself, Hugh, you'll turn out just like him.'

Hugh didn't think he deserved being tarred with the same brush as his father. 'I never promise marriage, Mum. Or children. I'm honest with the women I sleep with.' He'd been *extremely* honest with Kathryn.

'That doesn't stop them getting emotionally involved. I really feel sorry for Krystal. I know you thought she was just another gold-digger. And, of course, ageing billionaires are often pursued for their money, not themselves. But your father is an impressive and very charming man. Plus extraordinarily good in bed, even at his age.'

Hugh stared at his mother. 'How on earth do you know that? Are you saying that you still *sleep* with him?'

A faint flush came to her cheeks. 'Only when he's between wives.'

'Good grief.'

'I've never stopped loving your father, Hugh,' she said without a shred of shame. 'I don't think I ever will. But my feelings are not the issue here. I think Krystal loved him too, and wanted to have children with him. She's only thirty-five, after all. Most women want to have at least one baby, Hugh. Kathryn is how old?'

'She'll be thirty next month.'

'Then her biological clock is ticking. This might sound harsh, Hugh, darling. You're my son and I love you dearly. But don't let that girl waste any more of her life on you. You won't ever give her what she wants.'

Hugh could have told her that he *was* actually giving Kathryn what she wanted. Lots of loving, plus the house up at Pearl Beach.

But he could appreciate what his mother was saying.

In hindsight, Kathryn *had* been different with him this morning. The way her eyes had lit up when he'd arrived at the office had delighted him at the time. His mother's words of warning, however, brought some common sense to the situation. Hadn't Kathryn herself told him that she always fell in love with a man if she enjoyed sleeping with him?

It was patently obvious that she was enjoying going to bed with him. She'd done exactly as he'd asked last night, met him at the door with nothing on but her high heels, after which they'd spent the next few hours playing erotic games. She'd delighted him with her surprise, and her surrenders. He'd loved teaching her new pleasures and had wallowed in her willingness to give him her whole body to explore and enjoy. By the time he'd taken her home, he was more enamoured with her than ever.

The thought of giving her up in a few weeks did not sit well with him.

Of course, there was another alternative. He could tell Kathryn he'd fallen in love with her and offer her a real marriage. Offer to give her children. That way, she would be his for a lot longer than a few weeks.

Hugh suspected she might not say no.

It would be easy to persuade her.

Easy…but not kind.

Because it would be a lie, the same kind of lie James had told Megan. And look where that had led. The reason for his marrying no longer existed and he was devastated. So was poor Megan. When she'd finally woken up yesterday from the sedation the doctor had given her, the grief in her eyes had been terrible to see. She'd banished everyone from her room, even her husband. He could still hear the sound of her heart-broken sobbing. It had been ghastly.

He and Russ had taken James down to the pub for a few drinks and a meal, and whilst they'd tried hard to comfort him, he'd refused to be comforted. In the end, Hugh had left Russ to it and come home to Kathryn, her nakedness soon driving all thought of his friend's despair from his mind.

But there was no ignoring reality when he was sitting opposite his mother and hearing about his father's latest failure to make a relationship work. Had Dickie offered Krystal children when he'd proposed? Had he promised to give her everything when all he'd really wanted was sex on tap with a woman young enough to be his daughter?

Probably.

Hugh had always believed he wasn't like his father.

The truth was he'd been afraid all his life that he was just like his father. That he couldn't love any woman enough to stay with her. That he couldn't love a child enough to be a decent father.

He was afraid that he was what he'd once told Kathryn, that he was selfish to the core.

But he wasn't, he suddenly realised. Not to the core. Because if he was, he'd take what Kathryn had to offer for as long as it pleased him and throw her away, the way his father had thrown his mother away.

But he wasn't going to do that. He was going to be kind. He was going to let Kathryn go.

Her eyes lit up again when he arrived back at the office around one-forty. She was looking particularly delicious today, dressed in a stunning white suit which he'd never seen on her before. Hugh suspected she'd taken extra trouble because of him. Which was another good reason for him to do what he was going to do.

'That's the shortest lunch with your mother that you've ever had,' she said. 'Wasn't the food any good?'

'So-so.' He walked over and sat down in one of the large armchairs which dotted the reception area. 'You haven't heard from Elaine by any chance, have you?'

'No. But I've only just got back from lunch myself. Why do you ask?' she said, and began checking the computer for mail.

'Apparently, Dad's latest marriage is down the drain and he's on his way home.'

Her eyes shot over to his. 'You're kidding me.'

'I kid you not,' he returned coldly. 'Well?'

'Yes, there's an email here from Elaine. And yes…you're right. Your father will be back in Sydney tomorrow, and back here, in his office, on Monday.'

'It would have been polite for him to tell me this himself,' Hugh said through gritted teeth.

'He might have tried. Is your mobile turned on?'

Hugh fished it out, then swore. He'd turned it off when he was at the hospital yesterday and hadn't thought to turn it back on.

'Can *you* ring *him*?' Kathryn suggested.

'Frankly, I'd rather not talk to him just now. I might say something I'll regret.' Though perhaps it was about time. He'd been biting his tongue where his father's multiple marriages were concerned for way too long.

'Should I ring Peter?' Kathryn asked. 'Tell him you'll be back in your own office, come Monday.'

Peter had been filling in for him whilst he'd been filling in for his father. A past editor of several of Parkinson's best-selling magazines, Peter was a very smart guy, extremely ambitious and totally dedicated to the company.

'No,' he said slowly. 'No, don't do that.'

'Why not?'

'Because I'm not going to go back to my office.'

'You're not?'

'No. Come Monday, I'm going to resign.'

'Resign!'

'Yes. I've decided that it's time I went my own way.'

'But…but…what will you do?'

'I'm not sure yet. I'll have to think about it. I don't need my father's money to survive, Kathryn. I have plenty of my own.'

'But what about me? I mean…I won't have a job if you resign!'

'I'll make sure you're well looked after,' he said. 'Don't worry. You'll have a fabulous reference, a terrific retrenchment package and, of course, by then you'll have that very important piece of paper: a marriage certificate.'

But I won't have *you*, Kathryn thought wildly as she looked over at him.

Oh, God, she was going to cry!

Jumping up, she practically ran to the powder room, where she stayed till she had herself firmly under control once more.

Hugh was waiting for her at her desk when she emerged, his own eyes worried as they scanned her face.

'I'm sorry, Kathryn,' he said, and took her hands in his. 'I didn't mean to upset you. But if you think about, you'll see it's all for the best.'

'I don't know what to think any more,' she said truthfully.

He smiled a small and rather rueful smile. 'I can appreciate your confusion. It's been one hell of a week. But we both knew that it wasn't going to last. I don't regret any of it. Do you?'

As she looked deep into his beautiful blue eyes, Kathryn knew without a doubt that she loved him. It wasn't just the sex, it went deeper than that. What she felt for Hugh was way different from what she'd felt for Daryl.

But there was no point in saying so. No point in trying to cling on to him. She could see the writing on the wall. Come Monday, they would part company and, except for perhaps a brief meeting with his solicitor in a few months' time when she filed for divorce, they would have no more to do with each other.

His words just now indicated that their affair was over.

Kathryn suddenly felt foolish that she'd worn the white suit today: she'd been going to wear it at her wedding to Daryl.

There'd been no special significance in this last act. She'd chosen to wear it simply because she knew she looked great in it. She'd fantasised about Hugh taking one look at her today and wanting her like crazy again. She'd imagined him sweeping her into his arms and taking up where he'd left off last night.

He'd given her the impression this morning that this might be on the cards—he'd certainly looked at her with desire in his eyes—but fate had intervened with Peter dropping by to see him first thing, after which Hugh had had phone calls and visitors all morning.

By the time his mother had arrived shortly before twelve-thirty, they hadn't had a single private moment together. A frustrated Kathryn had found it difficult to be at ease with Mrs Parkinson, her conversation feeling stilted. She'd been relieved when Hugh had finally left with her, though spending time alone hadn't been conducive to relaxation.

Images of the previous evening kept popping into her head, only the thought that she genuinely loved Hugh making her feel better about all they'd got up to. Surely it wasn't wrong to give yourself so totally to a man if you loved him.

It hadn't seemed wrong at the time. It had been very exciting. Very…fulfilling.

It was going to be extremely difficult to forget him.

Though why should I forget Hugh? came the defiant thought.

He'd been good to her, hadn't he? He'd given her Val's house, plus more sexual pleasure this past week than she'd experienced during her whole life so far.

At the same time, however, she didn't want to spend the rest of her life pining for Hugh. She needed to make a life for herself which would carry her through to old age. She wanted a family of her own. A husband and children to love and care for, and who would do the same for her.

As much as she might like to think he could be, Hugh would never be that man.

'Kathryn?' Hugh prompted, his voice sounding a tad anxious. 'You haven't answered me. You don't regret going to bed with me, do you?'

'No,' she said simply and sincerely. 'No, I don't regret it at all.'

'That's good. I'm glad. Now, I suppose I'd better contact all the section heads and let them know that my father will be back on deck next week. They've probably been slacking it with me in charge,' he added with a wry smile, turning away and heading for the door.

Clearly, he meant to transmit this news in person, not by phone or email.

'What do you want me to do whilst you're gone?' Kathryn asked.

Hugh stopped and turned. 'Nothing for me. You could give Elaine a ring. Find out if there's anything you need to do before Dad's return. Other than that, I suggest you pack up anything of yours from this office and go home. If I don't see you again today, I'll ring you tonight and make final arrangements for Sunday. Which reminds me, Russ is going to ask his wife, Nicole, to be the other witness. He said James needed to be with Megan, twenty-four-seven. And I agreed with him. But don't worry,' he threw over his shoulder as he whirled and strode off. 'Nickie won't breathe a word to anyone.'

Kathryn wasn't worried about that. What worried her was how she was going to cope, after Monday.

The future had often seemed black to her in the past, but never as much as at that moment...

CHAPTER SEVENTEEN

'I NOW pronounce you man and wife.'

Nicole's hand tightened around Russell's. Oh dear, she thought. What a tragedy this wedding was.

There was Hugh, the darling man, marrying his PA so that she could inherit some silly house. Yet it was perfectly obvious to anyone who knew him that Hugh was madly in love with this woman. Russell already thought so, and, now, so did she.

Hugh was so gentle with her. So...tender. Whereas she was cool to him, very cool.

It made Nicole want to cry.

'You may kiss the bride,' the minister added, a little unsurely.

Nicole wasn't sure what Hugh had told the poor man about this wedding but he clearly knew it wasn't entirely truthful.

When Hugh bent to give his PA a platonic peck on her cheek, his eyes were uncharacteristically bleak, confirming what Russell had told her last night; that this was undoubtedly the girl Hugh had been fancying for some time and who wouldn't come across.

Kathryn Hart wasn't beautiful in the traditional sense. But Nicole could see that lots of men would find her very sexy. She had an interesting face, a highly sensual mouth and a voluptuous figure which was at odds with her cool grey eyes and composed manner. Nicole could well understand Hugh being intrigued by her, especially if she'd shown not one whit of interest in him. He was used to women falling all over him.

If Hugh thought this marriage would get his PA into his bed, then he was mistaken. That girl didn't give a damn about him, or this marriage. It was just a means to an end where she was concerned.

Nicole would have loved to know why this beach house meant so much to her. She'd asked Russell but he was none the wiser.

Maybe one day she'd ask Hugh herself. But not today, she thought as she glanced at Hugh's far too serious face.

No, not today.

Not long to go now, Kathryn told herself as she signed the marriage certificate.

She gripped the pen tightly to prevent any telltale trembling, determined not to let anyone know that, inside, her heart was breaking. Kathryn had long perfected the art of presenting a coolly composed façade to the world. What you saw was not what she was. She'd managed well so far today, but it was beginning to be a struggle, especially with Nicole's cold green eyes upon her.

Russell McClain's wife was exactly what Kathryn would expect the wife of one of Hugh's wealthy friend to look like: too stunningly beautiful for words, her supermodel looks reinforcing what Kathryn already knew—that Hugh's sexual obsession for her had been some kind of temporary aberration, brought on by his being in constant contact with her, plus her not showing any visible interest in him.

Maybe, if she'd looked like Nicole McClain, she'd have stood a chance of ensnaring his love, as well as his lust.

But that was all water under the bridge now.

I should be grateful for small mercies, Kathryn thought as she handed the pen to the best man. I've at least had the experience of truly falling in love and being made love to by a man who, if not in love with me, wanted me so much he was prepared to marry me to have me.

The fact that his unlikely passion had waned before the actual wedding was irrelevant. He'd kept his word and still done the deed. Val's house was hers now.

Perversely, having Val's house didn't seem quite so important any more.

Like some kind of automaton, Kathryn went through the process of shaking the minister's hands and thanking him politely. Hugh did likewise before walking the man to the door, where he pressed an envelope into his hands, Kathryn wondering how much it had cost Hugh to buy the man's silence.

'As I told you last night, Russ,' Hugh said after the minister was gone, 'we're not having any kind of celebration. I really appreciate your being here. Both of you,' he added with a sweet smile Nicole's way. 'I don't want to rush you out, but I have some important things I have to discuss with Kathryn which really shouldn't wait.'

'That's perfectly all right,' his friend replied. 'Nickie and I understand. Good luck to you, Kathryn, with the house. And with the future.'

'What important things?' an instantly nervous Kathryn asked as soon as the front door closed and they were alone.

'Would you like some coffee first?'

'No,' she replied shortly.

'Very well,' he said, and drew another envelope out of his suit jacket pocket. 'This is not your official retrenchment package. That will be deposited in your bank account as soon as it can be properly organised by the human-resources department. This is from me. Personally.' And he handed her the envelope.

She stared at it as if it were a cobra about to strike. 'I don't want it!'

'You *do* want it,' he insisted, ripping open the envelope and extracting what looked like a cheque. 'This will set you up for life, if it's carefully invested. I know you plan to get married and have children. But even the best plans in life can be scuttled. Your future husband might get sick, or die, or leave you. This way, you'll always have your own money. You'll always be secure.'

Kathryn knew he was making sense, and that if she refused she was acting like some proud fool.

'Think of your children,' he argued when she still hesitated. 'You won't want them to ever suffer what you suffered as a child. You'll want them to always be safe and secure. Money can do that, Kathryn. Yes, I know money can't buy happiness, or love. But it can make misery a lot more comfortable. I know that for a fact,' he finished, and smiled a smile unlike any smile she'd ever seen Hugh smile. It was so sad, and bitter.

'All right,' she said, and took the cheque.

It was for two million dollars.

'There are two more things,' Hugh said.

Kathryn wasn't sure if she could bear much more. Tears were hovering, which made her say, 'What?' in a very short tone.

'First, there's no need for you to come into the office on Monday. I won't be there.'

'OK,' she agreed wearily. 'What else?'

'Put that cheque and the marriage certificate in your handbag and come with me.'

He took her down to the car park and over to where he always parked his Ferrari. Next to it was a sporty little white sedan, obviously brand-new.

Kathryn's heart turned over as she stared at it.

'I thought of buying you a real sports car,' Hugh said with one of his more familiar smiles, 'but decided that might attract the wrong kind of guy. So I settled on this.' He picked up her spare hand and dropped a set of keys in it. 'It's already in your name, registered and insured. The papers are in the glovebox.'

She could not stop the tears filling her eyes now.

'Oh, Hugh,' was all she could say.

'Don't,' he grated out. 'Please don't. I feel bad enough as it is.'

Her shimmering eyes lifted to his. 'There's no need to.'

'I beg to differ. Now just go, will you? Go, and don't look back.'

She stared after him as he stalked off.

Maybe she was wrong. Maybe he did care for her after all.

Just not the way she wanted him to care for her.

Driving back to her flat was difficult, with tears flooding her eyes at intervals. Once, she almost turned round and drove back to Hugh's place. But what would she say to him?

'I love you and I want to stay married to you.'

The thought of the appalled look on his face put paid to that stupid idea.

By the time she got to Ashfield, Kathryn knew what she had to do and where she had to go. Half an hour later, she was on her way to Pearl Beach.

CHAPTER EIGHTEEN

HUGH was slumped in a chair on his balcony, staring out to sea and seeing absolutely nothing. Not with his eyes, anyway. Inside his mind he was still seeing Kathryn, driving off with tears in her eyes.

Had he waited too long? Did she think she'd fallen in love with him?

Hugh couldn't bear the thought that he might have broken her heart. She'd had so much unhappiness in life. She deserved to be happy.

He should never have done what he'd done. He should have just married her as an act of kindness, then sent her on her way. To blackmail her into his bed made him as unconscionable as his father. That she'd enjoyed making love did not excuse him. If anything, it made him feel even guiltier. He'd taken advantage of her vulnerability and exploited her highly sexed nature. When she'd warned him of the risk that she might fall for him, what had he done? Ignored her warning then ruthlessly used her body for his own egotistical gratification and sexual pleasure.

He was a bastard of the first order.

Like father, like son.

This last thought struck a real nerve. Hell no, he wasn't that bad. He did have a kind streak. And a conscience.

His home phone ringing brought a sigh to his lips.

Rising slowly to his feet, he trudged inside to answer it.

'Hugh Parkinson.'

'It's only me, Hugh.'

Hugh sank down into the sofa next to the phone table. 'Hi Russ. What's up?'

'Are you alone?'

'Yep.'

'I thought as much. She's gone, hasn't she?'

'Yep.'

'So things didn't work out like you hoped.'

'What do you mean by that?'

'Come on, buddy, you don't have to lie to me. I figured it all out. She was the girl you fancied last year who wouldn't come across.'

'Yep.'

'But it's become more than fancying, hasn't it? You've fallen for her.'

Hugh was about to deny it when he pulled himself up short. He'd had several more of those emotional moments with her, a couple of times when they *hadn't* been in bed. The reverend pronouncing them man and wife had produced intense feelings in him, as had giving her that car.

Even so, Hugh was still not convinced that it was true love he felt, let alone the kind of love which lasted.

Not that it mattered now. Nothing mattered now.

'Maybe,' he said.

'No maybe about it, buddy. Nicole watched you with her today and she's quite sure.'

Hugh had to laugh. 'Then she knows more than I do. It's probably just sex, Russ.'

'How can it be just sex when you haven't slept with her?'

'Hell, Russ, you know me better than that, surely.'

'You *have* been sleeping with her?' Russ asked in shocked tones.

'Ever since I offered to marry her.'

'Well, I'll be damned!'

'I think it's me who'll be damned, Russ. Unconditional sex was my part of the bargain.'

'I don't know whether to admire you or admonish you. Not that I can judge. I wasn't Mr Goody-Two-Shoes when I first met Nicole.'

'You certainly weren't,' Hugh pointed out drily.

'So where is she now? Why aren't you collecting some more of your bargain? After all, Kathryn has to stay married to you till she inherits that house, doesn't she?'

'Technically. Look, I decided it was time to call it quits, OK? I'd had enough.'

'Enough sex, or enough of your conscience? No, don't bother to answer that. It would have been your conscience.'

Hugh sighed. 'You know me too well.'

'I do indeed. So what was she like in bed? She's not my type but I can see the appeal.'

'I've never been a kiss-and-tell kind of guy, Russ.'

'Since when? Oh, come on, have pity on me. Give me a hint.'

'Sorry.'

'OK. Be Mr Noble. Now on to the second reason for this call. Would you like to come over for dinner tonight? Nicole thought you might be feeling a little down.'

'I don't think so, Russ.'

'I told her you wouldn't come. So what are you going to do?'

'Not sure. I might get drunk.'

'Don't do that. Go out somewhere. Get back on the horse, buddy. Move on.'

'You're probably right.'

'I am right. You know what they say—the king is dead, long live the king.'

'That's a bit heartless, isn't it?'

'What's the alternative? Staying home and drinking yourself into oblivion? Or maybe you'd like to go to a psych and have analysis?'

'I'm not a therapy kind of guy, either.'

'You're certainly not. You're a man of action, Hugh. Now, get off your butt and do something.'

Hugh smiled a wry smile. 'You really know how to cheer up a person.'

'I've had a lot of practice this week. I said much the same to James yesterday.'

'And did it work?'

'He's going to convert the pool house into an art studio for Megan. Give her something to take her mind off the miscarriage. Then, when the time is right, he's going to take her on a second honeymoon.'

'Sounds like a good plan.'

'So what's *your* plan? And don't say you're not a planning kind of guy. The time has finally come for you to give the future a bit more thought. You're not getting any younger.'

'Meaning?'

'Meaning you should find out what you really want in life and go after it before you're too old.'

Hugh sat thinking about Russ's words, long after he'd hung up the phone. The trouble was, he finally accepted, he'd never aspired to any great goals, other than to not to make the same mistakes his father had made. Which was why he'd steered clear of greed, and the desire for power. And, oh, yes, love and marriage.

His easy-come, easy-go attitude to life and the opposite sex had worked for him till he'd met Kathryn. He'd been happy. Or as happy as any son of Dickie Parkinson could be. With Kathryn now gone, there was no reason why his old lifestyle shouldn't work for him again.

But somehow, being a playboy had lost its appeal.

Yet what was the alternative?

In the end he stood up and made his way into the bedroom, where he'd left his mobile phone. Picking it up, he rang the telephone assistance line. After they'd located a particular lady's number, Hugh steeled himself, then rang it.

'Kandi Freshman,' a woman's voice answered.

'Hi there, Kandi. It's Hugh. Hugh Parkinson.'

'Hugh! Oh, my goodness,' she trilled brightly. 'Fancying hearing from you after all this time. I thought I must have done something wrong.'

'Not at all. I've just been very busy.'

'Yes, I did hear you'd taken over from your father for a while.'

Hugh gritted his teeth. Why he was doing this, he had no idea. He didn't want to go out with Kandi. But neither did he want to stay home, alone.

'I was wondering if you'd like to go somewhere tonight.'

'Tonight? Oh! Well, I did have a date…but no worries,' she rushed on. 'I can cancel it.'

Hugh glanced at his watch. It was getting on for seven. A bit late to cancel a date.

But it was never too late when you had the chance of going out with a billionaire, he thought ruefully. When big money called, girls like Kandi dropped everything and came running.

Hugh couldn't imagine Kathryn ever doing anything like that. That was what he admired so much about her—her lack of greed, plus the strength of her character. She had courage, yet underneath she was touchingly fragile and sweet.

Russ had said to him to find out what he really wanted in life. Well, what he really wanted, Hugh realised with a rush of fierce resolve, was Kathryn. He knew that now. Knew it as surely as he knew he didn't want to be with a girl like Kandi ever again!

'Don't cancel your date for me,' he told her firmly.

'Oh, but—'

'No, no. I wouldn't want to be responsible for disappointing another man. Have fun,' he said, and hung up.

Five minutes later he was in his car, speeding towards Ashfield.

She wasn't there. Hugh knew where she'd gone even before a nosey neighbour informed him that Kathryn had been home earlier, but had left some time back 'in a snazzy new white car'.

A disappointed Hugh didn't have to be Einstein to know where she'd gone. That she'd fled to Pearl Beach, however, did have its positive side. Kathryn went there for solace, which meant she needed solace. Why? Hopefully because she'd fallen in love with him. Or at least thought she had.

Either way, it gave him hope.

Hugh considered ringing her mobile but decided against it.

For what would he say to her? I've discovered that I really love you and I want you back.

She might not come. Even if she thought she'd fallen in love with him, she might not want to stay married to him. He was, in her words, an arrogant, lazy, spoiled, selfish playboy with nothing to offer her except his money and a few well-practised skills in the bedroom department.

Not enough.

He needed more.

Russ had been so right. For what he needed was a plan.

Hugh smiled at this last thought. Having a plan and executing it should appeal to Kathryn.

Of course, it couldn't be too long a plan. He didn't trust her not to start putting her own plans into action and find some guy who would love her and marry her and give her children.

Just the thought of her marrying some other guy almost killed him. Still, she couldn't really do that yet. After all, she was still married to him, and had to stay married till she was thirty.

That was a month away.

So he had a month. A month to provide proof that he was a man of substance, someone she could respect and rely on. Already, ideas were tumbling into his mind. Suddenly, he felt re-energised. He could hardly wait for tomorrow to come to start putting his plan into action.

No, he wouldn't wait till then. Russ could help him with a couple of his ideas straight away.

He quickly found Russ's number in the menu of his mobile and rang it.

'Russell McClain,' came his friend's businesslike answer.

'Russ. It's Hugh. Is that dinner invitation still open?'

'Of course.'

'I'll be right over.'

CHAPTER NINETEEN

KATHRYN emerged from the gently waving water after a half-hour's solid swim, sat down on her towel with a sigh and stared blankly out to sea.

She went swimming every day these days, twice a day, the exercise achieving much more than the gym ever had. The ancient cheval mirror in Val's bedroom showed her she looked good, her body toned, her skin clear and lightly tanned. And whilst, generally speaking, she was happy with her life here at Pearl Beach, this Wednesday morning she was having a real struggle with low spirits. It was, after all, her thirtieth birthday and she had no one to celebrate it with.

Her neighbours were probably very nice people, but old habits died hard, and Kathryn hadn't attempted anything more so far than a wave and a smile. She wasn't one of those people who made friends easily. She spent her spare time swimming, walking, reading, watching TV and answering job ads in the local papers.

Hugh had been right when he'd said she wouldn't find anything quite as exciting as being his PA up here on the coast, but a high-profile, well-paying position was no longer Kathryn's priority. She didn't need a big salary to survive—not with two million dollars in the bank. Any job, however, would bring her into contact with other people, namely members of the opposite sex.

She'd had a couple of interviews last week but been told she was over-qualified. Over-qualified and over-every-damned-thing!

Oh, dear, she thought unhappily as she got up, shook her towel then began trudging across the sand towards Val's house.

No, *my* house, she amended in her mind. As of today.

Her head stayed down as she walked up the back path, her eyes looking at her bare feet, with their unvarnished toenails. She'd been meaning to paint them for ages, but hadn't been overly motivated.

'Penny for your thoughts.'

Her heart leapt as her eyes shot up to find Hugh standing on the verandah, leaning against the railing.

'Hugh! What on earth are you doing here?' Oh, God, he looked so gorgeous, despite only being dressed in jeans and a white T-shirt.

'I wanted to see how you were getting on. You're certainly looking well.'

Kathryn wasn't sure what to make of the way his eyes travelled over her bikini-clad body. Was that hunger in his gaze? Surely he hadn't come up here for some more sex. Surely not!

But what if he had?

Would she be able to resist him? *Could* she?

Her nipples immediately tightened, as did her belly.

Truly, she was hopeless where this man was concerned.

A quite savage burst of pride had her wrapping her rather large beach towel around her body, sarong-style, whilst she did her best to calm her racing heartbeat.

'I repeat,' she said coolly as she walked up the steps onto the verandah, 'what are you doing up here?'

'I've brought you a birthday present,' he said. 'It's over there, on that table.'

Any pleasure at his remembering her birthday was waylaid once she spotted the familiar paper parcel. 'I can't believe you came up all this way to give me a hamburger.'

'That's not the only reason for my visit.'

'If you've come for some more sex,' she threw at him defiantly, 'then you've made the trip for nothing.'

His smile was small and wry. 'That's not why I've come, either. Though you do look quite delicious in that itsy-bitsy bikini.'

A perverse wave of disappointment went crashing through Kathryn.

'I just wanted to talk to you,' he added.

The penny dropped. So did her galloping heartbeat. 'Oh I see. Now that I have legal possession of the house, you want me to file for divorce straight away.'

'Actually, no. That isn't why I've come, either. Look, why don't you eat your hamburger first? It's getting cold. Then we'll talk.'

Kathryn eyed him quite angrily. Who did he think he was, just showing up like this and upsetting her all over again? If he just wanted to talk about something, then why hadn't he phoned? He had her mobile number.

'The hamburger will have to wait, I'm afraid,' she said stroppily. 'I need to go have a shower and get this salt water out of my hair.'

'Fine. Would you mind if I used the bathroom first? It's been a long trip.'

Kathryn took the key from under the doormat and slipped it into the front-door lock.

'Wow,' Hugh said. 'That's some security system you have.'

'I only put it there during the short time I'm on the beach,' she told him sharply. 'It's better than losing the damned thing in the sand.'

'True. And it's not as though you have anywhere to put it on your person—not in that bikini you're almost wearing.'

'It's not that brief.'

'Maybe it just looks it on you.'

She rounded on him. 'Are you saying that I'm fat?'

'Lord, but you're touchy today,' he said with an amused smile. 'Of course you're not fat. You must know that. But you are well-endowed, shall we say?'

'You told me that my breasts were beautiful.'

'And they are.'

'Then shut up about my bikini being too small.'

'Yes, ma'am.'

'And don't start mocking me.'

'I'd forgotten how prickly you could be.'

'That's because you've probably gone back to dating your usual brand of sycophantic female.'

'Let's go inside, shall we?'

Hugh sat at the kitchen table, waiting for Kathryn to emerge from the bathroom. He'd collected the long-cold hamburger from the verandah and placed it on a plate next to the microwave. But he feared it was ruined. Feared his plan was ruined, also.

In his mind he'd imagined she'd be a lot happier to see him. He'd fantasised about her welcoming him with open arms. He should not have read so much into her tears the day of their wedding. That had to have been an emotional day for her. It didn't mean she had strong personal feelings for him, not the way he had for her.

At the same time, her being so angry with him just now

gave him some hope. Anger was not indifference. Neither was the way she'd looked at him during that split second when her eyes had lifted and she'd first seen him on her verandah.

Hugh was not above taking advantage of the sexual chemistry between them. Though that was not the way he wanted this to go today. It was not in his plan.

But when a man was as madly in love as he was with Kathryn…

Well…sometimes, you had to change plans midstream.

But first, he would try absolute sincerity. And brutal honesty.

'You could have at least made some coffee,' she snapped when she finally swept into the room, dressed in white Bermuda shorts and a cornflower-blue short-sleeved blouse which minimised her bust.

'I didn't think you'd want me rooting through your cupboards.'

'That's just an excuse,' she said, then busied herself putting on the kettle and setting out the necessaries for two mugs of coffee.

'Your hamburger's over there,' he pointed out.

'Yes, I can see that, Hugh. Sorry, but I don't feel like eating at the moment. I'll have it later. Now,' she said, leaning back against the pine cupboards and crossing her arms, 'you can start talking whilst we wait for the water to boil.'

Lord, but she could be terribly bossy, Hugh thought. Give her an inch and she'd take the proverbial mile. Though her ongoing stroppiness was very comforting.

She *did* care, he decided. It was just a matter of how much.

'I'd prefer to wait till you're sitting down. And I'd like a biscuit if you have one.'

Kathryn gritted her teeth but did as he asked, setting out a small plate of mixed creams and not saying another word till the coffee was made.

'Everything to your satisfaction, boss?' she said tartly as she pulled out the chair opposite him and sat down.

He smiled one of those warm, wonderful smiles which had helped him worm his way into her heart.

'Everything's perfect, Mrs Parkinson.'

Kathryn's heart lurched. 'Don't call me that,' she said, her voice not as sharp as she might have hoped.

'Why not?'

'I'm not your real wife.'

'Would you like to be?'

She just stared at him.

His eyes held hers, his coffee untouched. 'That is why I've come, Kathryn. To ask you to marry me again. Publicly next time...for real.'

Her mouth dropped open, then snapped shut. 'Why on earth would you want to do that?'

'I love you,' he said in an astonishingly sincere voice. 'I love you and I can't live without you.'

Oh, my God! Had he really just said that? It didn't seem possible, her natural cynicism battling against the tidal wave of joy his words evoked. 'But you always said that... that—'

'I know what I always said,' he cut in. 'But I was wrong. I love you, Kathryn Hart, with every fibre of my being.'

Kathryn put her hand over her heart as it threatened to jump right out of her chest.

'I tried to forget you after you left,' he went on whilst she still struggled to get her head around this amazing declaration. 'But you refused to be forgotten. I knew within hours of sending you away that my feelings for you weren't just lust.

I knew that true love had finally taken possession of my, till then, shallow soul.'

Kathryn simply could not find the right words of reply.

'Yes, I know,' he said with a wry smile. 'It came as a shock to me too. To suddenly come face to face with something as serious as true love has rocked my world, I can tell you.'

'You really, truly love me?' she blurted out at last.

'You'd better believe it, my darling.'

'Oh...' She cupped her cheeks as tears flooded her eyes.

'Dare I hope those tears mean you love me back?'

'You...you know I do,' she choked out.

'Hell, no! I didn't know any such thing!' He jumped up, his face beaming. He raced round the table and pulled her up into his arms.

'Tell me again,' he said fiercely. 'Say the words.'

'I love you,' she said, and blinked away the tears.

'Again,' he insisted.

'I love you,' she said more loudly.

His groan was a groan of sheer relief. 'I told Russ and Nickie the night after we married that I thought you might be in love with me.'

'Then why didn't you come after me straight away?'

'I wanted to, believe me. I went to your flat at Ashfield but you weren't there.'

'I'd come up here.'

'I realised that. I also realised I had to do something to prove to you that I wasn't a lazy, spoiled, arrogant jerk. I wanted to have more to offer you than money and sex. So for the last month I've worked my silver tail off, setting up a business of my own.'

Kathryn was truly taken aback. 'Really? What kind of business?'

'The only one I know well: publishing. But books this time, not magazines. Australia's got more than enough magazines, as you know. I'm going to publish fiction. We have loads of great writers in this country who don't ever get published. I'm going to give anyone with talent a chance. Then I'm going to take that talent to the whole world, show them what Aussie authors can do.'

'Oh, Hugh, that's a marvellous idea.'

'See? That's what I want to see in your eyes whenever you look at me: respect. So, will you come back to Sydney and help me?'

'You mean as your PA?'

'Hell, no. As my partner, both in business and in life! We'll have a big proper swanky wedding in a couple of months' time, with all the trimmings. It'll cost dear old Dad a fortune and make my mother happy at the same time. She's going to be over the moon when she finds out we're getting married. I'll get Reverend Price to officiate. He won't tell anyone it's a rerun.'

Kathryn laughed. 'You are crazy, you know that, don't you?'

'I've been crazy ever since you came into my life. That, I know. But I wouldn't have it any other way.'

'You wouldn't?'

'No.'

'Neither would I,' she said, her heart turning over. 'I love you, Hugh.'

'Just as well, because I spent a small fortune on this.' Out of his jeans pocket he drew a small box. A ring box.

'You can change it if you don't like it,' he said as he flipped the lid open.

Kathryn stared down at the most exquisitely beautiful diamond engagement ring. It wasn't too big, or too showy. And it wasn't gold.

'It's lovely,' she said. 'How did you know I prefer silver?'

'I'm not totally inobservant. But it's not silver, it's white gold.' He took it out of its blue velvet nest and slipped it on her ring finger. It fitted perfectly.

'How did you know what size to pick?'

'I didn't. I made an intelligent guess. There's a matching wedding ring, but you don't get to wear that one yet.'

'Oh, Hugh. I don't know what to say.'

'Then don't say anything.'

He kissed her then, after which he kissed her some more. They somehow made it into the main bedroom where their clothes were dispensed with at amazing speed.

Their lovemaking was fast and furious, neither of them stopping for breath till it was all over. Only then did Hugh speak.

'I didn't use a condom,' he said somewhat raggedly.

'I know.'

'You're still on the Pill, aren't you?'

'What would you say if I wasn't?'

'Yippee?'

'Wonderful answer,' she said with a smile on her face, and in her heart. 'But it's all right, I am.'

'That's good. I want our first child to be conceived within wedlock.'

'But Hugh, we're already legally married.'

'Yeah, but my parents don't know that. I don't want to be seen to be a chip off the old block, having impregnated my PA and then having to marry her. I've always believed that marriage should be entered into for love, of the deep and forever kind. When we exchange vows the next time, it will have so much more meaning.'

'I already loved you the last time.'

He shook his head. 'I don't know why.'

She reached up and stroked his cheek. 'Then you don't know women as well as you think you do. Now would you like to show me how much *you* love *me*, a little more slowly next time?'

'Yes, ma'am,' he said laughingly.

CHAPTER TWENTY

KATHRYN wasn't at all nervous.

She'd thought she would be. Thought she might be overwhelmed by the occasion.

Instead, she felt quite calm, and very very happy.

'You look absolutely divine!' Hugh's mother exclaimed. 'That wedding dress is just made for you.'

'Leonie,' Kathryn replied, amusement in her voice, 'it *was* made for me. And it cost a small fortune, as you very well know. You paid for it.'

Leonie, who was looking elegant and beautiful in pale blue, smiled back at her. 'No, dear, Dickie paid for it. Now, can I tell you a little secret?'

'Of course.'

The two women had become quite close during the run-up to the wedding, with Kathryn letting her future mother-in-law make all the arrangements. Partly because she'd been kept very busy over the past two months, helping Hugh with his new business. But mostly because Kathryn had been afraid she might embarrass Hugh—and herself—by penny-pinching. That was one thing she wasn't quite used to yet—having an unlimited budget.

'Dickie and I are going to get married again,' Leonie said in a conspiratorial whisper. 'As soon as his divorce comes through.'

'That's wonderful, Leonie. Hugh's going to be thrilled.'

'Oh, I doubt that, dear. Hugh can't understand why I still love his father. On top of that, he's never too thrilled with anything Dickie does. But you seem to like Dickie. I know he likes you.'

'He's a sweetie,' Kathryn said. And a scoundrel. And a flirt.

He'd insisted within five minutes of meeting Kathryn that she call him Dickie. And given her a sneaky pat on her backside when no one had been looking.

But he seemed genuinely fond of Leonie. And maybe, now that he was into his sixties, he might have finally seen the sense of having a wife more of his own age. A wife, more to the point, who genuinely loved him and who was the mother of his only son and heir.

'It was good of him to let us get married on his yacht,' Kathryn said.

'Sensible, too,' Leonie said. 'This way the paparazzi can't bother us too much.'

Dickie's superyacht—called *The Boadicea* for some reason—was moored in the middle of Sydney harbour, a few hundred metres out from his main residence, a huge water-side mansion at Darling Point. A ship of *The Boadicea*'s size required a reasonably deep anchorage, the wedding party and guests having been ferried out from Dickie's private pier by a smaller cruiser which the Parkinson family used for jaunts around the harbour. The ceremony was due to take place just before sunset on the biggest of the back decks, followed by a seated reception in the main saloon. There weren't all that many guests—around sixty—Hugh refusing to let his parents invite people he didn't personally like, or respect.

'Which eliminates most of your business associates,' he'd told his father.

Dickie had been extremely patient with him, in Kathryn's opinion. Patient and indulgent. He seemed genuinely pleased that his son was finally getting married. And secretly proud, Kathryn thought, that Hugh had decided to go out on his own into the business world.

Kathryn certainly was. Proud, and more in love with Hugh than ever. He stunned her sometimes with the creativity of his vision, and his new-found capacity for work. Some days, she had trouble keeping up with him.

Even so, he still had the energy to make love to her every night.

After her honeymoon, however, there would be no more pills. She wanted to have Hugh's children before she was too old to enjoy them.

'I'll just see if Nicole's ready yet,' Leonie said, and knocked on the door which connected the two rooms set aside for the bride and her bridesmaid, two rooms being necessary because the bedrooms on the yacht weren't all that large.

'We're ready in here, sweetie,' Leonie called through the door. 'How are you going?'

'Won't be a sec,' Nicole answered. 'My phone's ringing. Tell Kat not to panic. It doesn't matter if we're a little bit late. Hugh's not going anywhere.'

Kathryn smiled at Nicole calling her Kat, Hugh's nickname for her having already caught on with most of his friends.

Kathryn was still surprised by how much she'd taken to Russell's wife, and vice versa, Nicole having been very warm and welcoming after her return to Sydney with Hugh. It seemed only natural that Kathryn would invite Nicole to be her chief bridesmaid opposite Russell's best man. She would have asked James's wife to be a bridesmaid as well—and it would have been nice for Hugh to have his two best friends stand by his side at his wedding—but Hugh said James thought Megan wasn't up to it just yet.

Poor Megan. Apparently, she'd taken her miscarriage very hard, and rarely left the house any more. She hadn't done any socialising at all over the months since it had happened, James only just managing to persuade her to come to Hugh's wedding as a guest.

Kathryn felt very sorry for her.

The interconnecting door opened and Nicole walked in looking elegantly beautiful in the pale green evening gown which Leonie had chosen for her.

'Oh, you look so gorgeous!' Nicole exclaimed on seeing the bride in full regalia for the first time.

Kathryn knew that she would never be as stunning-looking as Nicole. But even she could see that today she looked pretty amazing, her designer-made wedding dress having a style which suited her hourglass figure to perfection. Her full breasts looked great in the strapless, tightly fitted diamanté bodice, which was overlaid with lace and studded with pearls. Her tiny waistline would have rivalled Scarlett O'Hara's, even without a corset to pull it in, though perhaps this was an illusion created by the dress's full and very feminine skirt.

Her hair and make-up had been attended to this morning by a top beauty salon in Double Bay, Kathryn very pleased with the end result. Her thick, glossy dark hair was up, but not severely, several softly curled strands framing her superbly made-up face. Her long lace-edged tulle veil was anchored by a simple row of small white roses, which matched her white rose bouquet. Small pearl drops hung from her ears and a single strand of Paspali pearls—a wedding present from Hugh—adorned her neck.

All in all, Kathryn knew she would never look better.

'Thank you,' she replied. 'You look pretty amazing yourself.'

'Green does suit me,' Nicole said. 'That was Russell on the phone just now. He said he can't believe how calm Hugh is. You've had a wonderful effect on him, Kathryn.'

'He's had a wonderful effect on me,' she said, thinking how Hugh's more easy-going nature had begun to rub off on her.

'Russell also said we should consider making an appearance soon,' Nicole added. 'He said if we were fashionably late, we might miss the sunset, which I'm told is one in a million today.'

'OK, I'll go get Max,' Leonie said.

'Max?' Nicole echoed when Leonie disappeared. 'Who's Max?'

Kathryn smiled. 'He's on the board of directors at Parkinson Media. The only one Hugh likes. Hugh asked him if he would give me away and he agreed.'

'How strange.'

'Not really. He's a nice man and I didn't have anyone else.'

Nicole's heart turned over at this sad state of affairs. She'd learned quite a bit about Kathryn over the last two months, though most of it had been from Hugh, not Kathryn herself.

Kathryn was not a girl who confided easily. She was a bit like Megan in that regard. Though Megan was more shy than wary.

From what Hugh had told Nicole, Kathryn had every reason to be less than trusting of people and friendship. But

Nicole could see a big change in Hugh's choice of wife over the past few weeks. She'd become much less uptight and a lot more open.

Max arrived, a tall, ruddy-faced, once-handsome gentleman in his late sixties. Nicole was glad when his attention was all for the bride, Max gushing and fussing over her before leading a beaming Kathryn out into the corridor.

Nicole exchanged wide smiles with Leonie. 'This is going to be a very happy day,' she said.

As Hugh stood on the deck, waiting for Kathryn to make an appearance, he wasn't quite as calm as Russell presumed. He felt impatient and somewhat irritated, mostly with his father, whose announcement a short while ago that he was going to remarry Hugh's mother as soon as it was legally allowed not sitting well with Hugh.

What in heaven's name was his mother thinking? It was one thing to sleep with his father, quite another to remarry him.

Hugh's stomach tightened as he watched his mother join his father in the first row of seats and give him a kiss on the cheek.

But then he caught sight of the happy glow on her face. And he recalled what Kathryn had said to him just the other day when he complained about his father's past behaviour.

'You can't really judge other people's actions, Hugh. You don't know what's happened in the past to make them what they are. You do love your father, despite everything, the same way I loved my mother, despite everything. Towards the end of her life, I finally stopped being bitter and accepted her for what she was; she's not a deliberately cruel person, just weak. It's time you accepted what your father is, warts and all. Time you forgave him as well.'

I'll try, Hugh thought, and immediately felt better.

'Oh, wow!'

Russell's admiration-filled exclamation snapped Hugh back to the present. But it wasn't the bride Russell was gaping at. It was his own wife, who admittedly looked exquisite in a softly draped green dress which fell right to the floor. She seemed to float down the strip of red carpet which ran between the rows of seats set up on the deck.

'Smile,' Nicole whispered to Hugh as she drew close, then moved to one side.

Hugh smiled just as the music started up, projected from several speakers positioned around the deck. It was the traditional bridal march, a stirring number which would have stirred Hugh, even if he hadn't at that moment been confronted with a sight which would remain emblazoned on his heart forever.

He'd always thought Kathryn beautiful. Beautiful inside and out. Today, however, she was beyond beauty. She was a Cinderella bride, wearing a dream dress, in a fairy-tale setting.

Tears pricked at his eyes as he watched her walk down the sun-drenched aisle with that wonderful composure which he'd always admired.

Hugh didn't bother to blink the tears away, knowing that only more would come. Straight from his heart, which was overflowing with love for her—love and gratitude.

For what would his life have become if she hadn't come along, if she hadn't loved him the way she did?

Hugh knew that Kathryn's love had healed him in ways he was still appreciating. He was no longer afraid of commitment, no longer drifting aimlessly in a never-ending sea. His life felt full of purpose, each day dawning with a rush of positive spirit, and pride.

Pride in himself. And her, this lovely and loving woman walking towards him.

The sight of Hugh's shimmering eyes stripped Kathryn of her calm.

'Oh, dear,' she choked out under her breath.

Max shot her a sharp look. 'If you cry, your make-up will be ruined,' he said swiftly. 'So will all the photographs.

'No crying allowed,' he went on, by then close enough for Hugh to hear. 'This is your wedding day, the happiest day of your life. And the smartest of yours, my boy,' he directed at Hugh as he handed the bride over to him.

Hugh smiled down at Kathryn, then turned her to face Reverend Price, who was standing behind a small podium, looking suitably serious in a dark grey suit.

'We are gathered here today,' the reverend started straight away, his last word totally drowned out when a helicopter suddenly swooped over them, 'to join this man and this woman in holy matrimony,' he added more loudly with a glare up at the sky when the helicopter returned, then hovered overhead.

The paparazzi, it seemed, had finally come to the wedding.

Hugh squeezed Kathryn's hand. 'Sorry about this,' he whispered. 'A hazard of marrying a Parkinson.'

She smiled up at him. 'I'll cope,' she said, knowing that she could cope with anything, if Hugh really, truly loved her.

Which he did.

'I know you will,' he said smilingly. 'But will Reverend Price?'

Both bride and groom had trouble keeping a straight face as the poor man got louder and louder in order to override the noise from above. Finally, the ceremony was over, with his proclaiming them man and wife in a decidedly hoarse voice.

'And now,' he practically squawked, 'you may kiss the bride.'

Everyone started to clap when Hugh did just that. By the time his head lifted, the helicopter had flown off and everyone heard Hugh say, 'I love you, Mrs Parkinson,' which brought another burst of applause.

'Nicole was right,' Leonie told Hugh's father with tears streaming down her face. 'This is, indeed, a very happy day…'

FREE!

2 Books
and a surprise gift!

We would like to take this opportunity to thank you for reading this Mills & Boon® book by offering you the chance to take TWO more specially selected titles from the Modern™ series absolutely FREE! We're also making this offer to introduce you to the benefits of the Mills & Boon® Book Club™—

- ★ **FREE home delivery**
- ★ **FREE gifts and competitions**
- ★ **FREE monthly Newsletter**
- ★ **Exclusive Mills & Boon Book Club offers**
- ★ **Books available before they're in the shops**

Accepting these FREE books and gift places you under no obligation to buy, you may cancel at any time, even after receiving your free shipment. Simply complete your details below and return the entire page to the address below. You don't even need a stamp!

YES! Please send me 2 free Modern books and a surprise gift. I understand that unless you hear from me, I will receive 4 superb new titles every month for just £3.19 each, postage and packing free. I am under no obligation to purchase any books and may cancel my subscription at any time. The free books and gift will be mine to keep in any case.

P9ZEF

Ms/Mrs/Miss/Mr ....Initials.................

BLOCK CAPITALS PLEASE

Surname ....

Address..

....

....Postcode...............

Send this whole page to:
UK: FREEPOST CN81, Croydon, CR9 3WZ